I0525853

AIRSHIP 27 PRODUCTIONS

Young Nemo and the Black Knights
© 2014 Michael Lail

Published by Airship 27 Productions
www.airship27.com
www.airship27hangar.com

Interior illustrations © 2014 Chuck Bordell.
Cover illustration © 2014 Rob Davis and Shane Evans
Editor: Ron Fortier
Associate Editor: Jerry Edwards
Marketing and Promotions Manager: Michael Vance
Production and design by Rob Davis.

ISBN-13: 978-0692340165 (Airship 27)
ISBN-10: 0692340165

Printed in the United States of America

10 9 8 7 6 5 4 3 2 1

by Michael Vance

Introduction

Captain Nemo was an Indian whose title and name at birth were Prince Rajesh Dakkar, son of the Rajah, or King, of the then independent territory of Bundelkund in central India. His father's name was Agnimukha, meaning "a face of fire", and the Prince was also a descendant of Sultan Fateh Aki Tipu of Mysore. His mother's name was Amala, which in Hindi means "pure, clean".

Dakkar was born on July 18th, 1818. He was born of average height and weight, perfect in health, with brown hair and large, grey eyes, but the word "average' would seldom be used to describe Rajesh throughout his life. At the age of three, Rajesh Dakkar began to read books. At five years of age, the evidence of his genius was overwhelming, and his father determined to feed the seed of his intellectuality with every means available to a Rajah. Those means were more than substantial.

His father employed a young man from Allahabed, India, whose own reputation for wisdom would spread across the nation. He had raised this man from a young age, saving him from a bleak life of squalor and poverty as an orphan. His name was Indra Singh, and his principal purpose was to mentor Rajesh and to secure the best tutors and materials for the instruction of his student.

In addition, the Rajah decreed that merchants who supplied his physical needs from around the world should also buy and bring to his mansion in Bundlekund any book they could find in their travels to stock a library for Dakkar. By Rajesh Dakkar's tenth birthday, his collection of books was already the largest in India.

Among his volumes were the scientific and philosophical writings of Aristotle and his Athenian School. The first translation of the Jewish Bible into Greek, accomplished at Alexandria by the Seventy and known as the Septuagint, was procured. The dark Necronomicon written by a mad Arab sat by this translation of the Bible. And all of the world's knowledge of science, religion, politics, history and myth were gathered by Singh for Prince Dakkar.

And yet, Dakkar's thirst for knowledge was unquenchable.

His father also understood the importance and demands of a healthy body to house his son's genius. Singh was instructed to teach Dakkar physical exercise, meditation, martial arts, and the science and art of yoga. Although Dakkar excelled at archery and wrestling, nothing could match the Prince's love for swimming. The river Ganges was his second home, and Singh often joked that Dakkar's real mother was a mermaid. It wasn't a great exaggeration. His mother was a beautiful, educated woman, well versed in the arts, especially music. She loved to play the piano.

Dakkar never understood the humor of the mermaid joke. He was too often too pragmatic for attempts at humor.

This aspect of Rajesh Dakkar's personality seemed to deepen with age, and Singh's concern over this weakness in his ward deepened as well. Dakkar seemed more interested in knowledge than in living life. He also loved mankind but disdained man, an unhealthy attitude at best.

In addition, Indra Singh had embraced Christianity through his upbringing, the exercise of reason, as well as through an act of faith. Dakkar found the idea laughable and a weakness in Singh. His constant derision of Singh's belief was a burr in his tutor's side and a thorn in his heart. But he kept the burr and thorn hidden for the most part. To heighten his disdain of religion and all traditions, Dakkar began to wear the symbol of low caste in India. The dot of caste remained constantly on Dakkar's forehead as a youthful act of rebellion. His father secretly liked the spirit of rebellion and allowed it.

By the time Prince Dakkar had reached nine years of age, it was painfully clear to Singh that he had exhausted Rajesh's father's and his own resources, and could teach Dakkar no more. With a deep sense of regret, he recommended Dakkar be sent away from India to complete his education at the great universities of Europe. Indra did not accompany his ward, and suffered a great loss from this decision because he had grown to love the boy as his own.

His father sent the prince, when ten years of age, to Europe, in order that he might receive an education in all respects complete and in the hope that by his talents and knowledge he might one day take a leading part in raising his long degraded and heathen country, India, to a level with the nations of Europe. Rajesh did not share his father's hope.

Dakkar would eventually travel over the whole of Europe. His rank and fortune caused him to be everywhere sought after by those who wanted wealth, power, or recognition, or by his peers who simply wanted to be near him, but the pleasures of the world had for him no attractions. Though young and possessed of every personal advantage, he was ever grave, somber even, devoured by an unquenchable thirst for knowledge and cherishing in the recesses of his heart the hope that he might become a great and powerful ruler of a free and enlightened people. He spent his leisure hours in libraries and scientific laboratories.

Still, for long the love of science triumphed over all other feelings. As a genetic gift from his mother, he became an artist deeply impressed by the marvels of art, as a genetic gift from his father, a philosopher to whom no one of the higher sciences was unknown. Later in life, he would become a statesman versed in the policy of European courts. To the eyes of those who observed him superficially, he might have passed for one of those cosmopolitans curious of knowledge but disdaining actions; one of those opulent travelers, haughty and cynical, who move incessantly from place to place, and are of no country. However, he was most often thought a snob.

This artist, this philosopher, this man, however still cherished the hope instilled into him from his earliest days. So, at the age of eighteen when he returned home, Dakkar bought a 150 ton brig with square rigged sails, christened it "Nautilus" after the Indian god of oceans, dramatically modified and improved the efficiency of the craft, and decided to set out to conquer the world.

He did not do so. The world, after all, objected.

Chapter One

Lincoln Island heaved and spasmed as the twin volcanoes that had created it eons ago erupted in raw, profane fury. The thunderous sound was deafening.

Instantly, a roaring, searing shock wave howled across the small, uncharted island, flattening or vaporizing almost everything organic in its path; trees, plants, animals, birds, and even insects. White-hot boulders and rocks and huge splotches of lava belched out of the red maws of the volcanoes to momentarily hang in the blistered air and then fall in a rain of scorching death to the earth. Then a drool of hellish lava, a liquid, molten ocean, began to vomit over the scorched lips of the volcanoes and beneath the spreading, moiling grey cloud of soot that would eventually smother everything it touched with a dirty slag. The air was violated with a nauseous stench.

The bay of the mysterious island heaved where the huge, metal Leviathan of the Oceans lay anchored, nine-tenths of its tonnage submerged beneath the waves. Then the waters of the bay touching the shores of the island convulsed and erupted in massive clouds of scalding steam as the first fiery fingers of lava that had laboriously stretched across the island's beaches cauterized sand into glass.

As the leviathan, the Nautilus, began to lurch in the first pangs of the tsunami born of the eruption, its hatch fell shut with a clang unheard in the chaotic roar of the volcanoes, the boiling waters of the bay, and the screaming winds. It was not the first time Captain Nemo had seen catastrophe.

Despite the turmoil above the sealed hatch over his uncovered head, the submarine's grey-bearded captain, wearing a hard-blue, double-breasted uniform, descended the metal rungs of a ladder to the first interior deck of the Nautilus on sea-legs steady with a certainty born from decades of life spent on the world's oceans. It was not his first experience with storms, literally or figuratively, in his long years of failure and triumph on the seas.

There were three gold bars embroidered above the wrists of each of his uniform's sleeves, and blue epaulets at each shoulder. His boots, dyed black, were of tanned whale skin, as was his belt. His was a uniform designed by his own hand and unduplicated by any other in the world.

The submarine's stabilizers that he'd invented did much to lessen the fury of the ocean above that, nevertheless, still tossed his ship from side to side as he walked, with single-minded focus, down a long, narrow hall decorated with amazing treasures that had lost their interest for him by familiarity. He passed the ship's library and its 12,000 volumes of books and manuscripts, some written by his own hand, before arriving at his stateroom filled with paintings and his large pipe organ. He did not look at the organ on its far wall or his shelves of personal books, many were rare first editions, as he passed. When he came to his stateroom, Nemo entered, moving without hesitation to his treasured roll-top, mahogany desk, scuffed and worn from much use; treasured because it was a birthday gift from his father. With the exception of his education in Europe, that desk had followed him wherever his unsaturated thirst for knowledge had led him. Yet it bore fewer scars than did he.

The Nautilus lurched. He steadied himself with his left hand on the side of the desk.

Nemo sat down in the desk's chair, bolted to the floor as were all the furnishings of the Nautilus. His face calm, resigned to the fury above that he did not create and could not control or stop, he rolled back its top and removed a small, rectangular box on the workspace of the desk sitting behind an open book and next to his feathered, quill pen. On the lid of the box was a raised shield bearing an oddly shaped letter somewhat like an N. Opening it, the sixty-six year old man poured out a handful of sepia-toned photographs; markers of a life that almost seemed a dream now.

From the disarray of memories; of images of his mother cradling him when a very young boy, of his father, a middle-aged man dressed as an Indian Rajah, of his mother, his father, the Rajah, and himself in his teenaged years, the old seafarer chose a photograph of a man dressed in a robe called a lungis standing in front of a magnificent Indian palace; his father's palace. As he looked at the picture, tears welled up in his weary, blue eyes. He said one word. "Singh," with a longing for something precious lost and a weariness born from interminable years of labor. No one answered.

He placed the thumb of his right hand on his cheek and cupped his chin with the remaining fingers. The fingernails were meticulously manicured.

Above him, the island was rocked by a deafening and severe explosion. With growing and conscious effort to steady himself in his chair against the increasing pitch and lurch of the submarine, the old man laid the photograph on his desk, removed the quill pen from its anchored ink well, and began to write about the beginning of a young man's first expedition and the handpicked men who became his Black Knights, about the tragic losses and the long years of hardships that followed that adventure, about hatred, joy and humiliation, and wrote knowing with certainty that these were the first of the last words that would ever be added to this last of many diaries.

Diary of the Nautilus. 1884. Lincoln Island. Dakkar Grotto. South Pacific.

I have lived for sixty-six years, devoured by an unquenchable thirst for knowledge. Many have hailed me as the penultimate genius of my age; more have called me the Great Satan. I call myself a failure.

I debated philosophy with the highest minds of science, and hoarded masterpieces of art from man and nature. My wealth is immeasurable. Yet I have failed to end war. I have failed to find a new way to feed the starving of the world.

The ruins of Atlantis have crumbled beneath my feet. From the belly of this metal fish I call Nautilus, I slew thousands who sought to slay tens of thousands.

Yet I am a man of no country or time; of all mankind, I am the most wretched and alone.

It was not always so for a Prince who is now feared and hated as Nemo.

In 1828, at the age of ten, my father sent me from the independent territory of Bundelkund, India, to Europe. At its universities, I was to receive an education in all things complete. But, having learned all that was available, I returned home still starved for knowledge.

In 1836, I left Bundelkund, restless and haughty; to find answers to questions few men even dare to ask. I was eighteen...and determined to lay bare the great secret. Of what price is demanded of a man to gain the whole world. Of what he must lose.

March, 1818. Bundlekund, India.

The crude, wooden door to the small house burst open, slamming against its anchor wall.

Ten men, women, and children of different ages and all dressed in the rags of poverty jerked around to see twelve Hindus, heavily armed with drawn swords, sheathed knives, and raised clubs, erupt across the threshold of the breached door, yelling and cursing.

Several women screamed. Children buried their faces in the bosoms of their mothers.

A thirteenth thug who carried a lit torch blocked the doorway with his body.

A fraction of a second passed and the pastor of the tiny congregation who faced the goons stood up from his chair, leaned down, and calmly said to the startled seven-year-old boy seated next to him who was his son, "Run! Hide! Now!"

The little boy jumped up out of the chair as the room became a chaos of movement and sound, his face flushed with fear and question and confusion, and ran to an open interior doorway opposite the thugs, and the third person on the couch who was his mother clasped her hands together, bowed her head, and began to pray as her body shook with terror.

In the third second, the pastor stood immobile, waiting, as the obvious leader of the armed men walked directly to him. The seven other members of his congregation moiled like ants, some instinctively trying to escape, some standing in defiance, and others shielding someone with their bodies from what they thought was certain death.

In the fourth second, the pastor said to the leader of the armed men who were now pushing, and slapping, and beating his congregation, "Hello, Nirmal Das. Please...don't do this."

"Go to Hell, Singh," Nirmal Das answered. "Here, let me help you," and he raised the sword he carried and drove its blade *thuck* through the pastor's body.

In the sixth second as the pastor slumped to the floor, dead, one of the thirteen thugs beheaded the praying woman, another clubbed a man trying to shield his head with his arms who collapsed to the floor as a woman, most likely his wife, grabbed the thug's arm in a vain attempt to stop him, he shook here off like a rag doll, and a third thug stabbed a woman pleading for the life of her baby in the heart.

By the tenth second, nine members of the house church lay dead or near death.

Breathing heavily as were his men, and listening to the moans of the dying, the mob's leader looked around the room at his fellow murderers and the disarray of bloody bodies, and said, "Vishnu smiles on us today. Now, my brothers, the stakes."

In the closet where he crouched, the little boy shivered and wept, his hands over his mouth to stifle the sound of his sobbing, and listened to muffled words and shuffling feet, and the scraping sounds of something being drug across the floor, until silence fell like a blanket over the house.

Overwhelmed with fear and confusion, he did not move. He could not move as minutes that felt like years fell into the blanket of silence and disappeared. He crouched and asked in his head what was happening, and why it was happening, and what should he do, and when would his father or mother find him, and why didn't God stop it.

He crouched and shivered and wiped the tears from his eyes with the heels of his trembling hands as the scraping and talking fell apart and drifted out of the house.

He did not know what to do, so he did nothing.

Slowly, he heard more scraping and talking far away, he knew now with certainty that is was near but somewhere outside of the house, and very small. Then minutes became ten, and then fifteen, and then he smelled it.

It was smoke.

Smoke made no sense, so he continued to do nothing but shiver, and whisper a little prayer as the smell grew stronger and stronger and he had to put a hand over his mouth to stifle a cough, and there were new, louder sounds, still muffled, now inside the house again. Surely it was his father.

The closet door was jerked open.

He looked up, terror in his eyes.

The man in the yellow turban and blue uniform who carried a sword yelled to someone else, not him, "Over here! Here's one!"

The man sheathed his sword, knelt before him, and said, "Have no fear, little one, you are safe. I am of the Royal Guard of the King of Bundlekund," and picked him up off the floor. He stood up, holding the little boy against his chest with his left arm, and gently forced his head down on his shoulder with his right, gloved hand on the back of his head.

"I am taking you out of the house," he said calmly. "But I need your help. The house is on fire. You must close your eyes as tight as you can, and not open them until I tell you to. Can you do that?"

The little boys nodded within the confines of the guard's restraining hand and said, "Where's my dad and mother?"

"I don't know, son," the guard lied. "Promise?" asked the guard. "Cross your heart?"

The little boy nodded again.

Then in less than twenty steps, the little boy knew that they were outside the house and moving more deeply out into the street that was in front of the home church.

The little boy felt the guard stop, turn, and kneel, putting him on the ground. The guard's hands remained firmly on his shoulders so that he could not turn around. Then he heard:

"Open your eyes, little one. You are safe now, and there's someone who wants to meet you."

The seven-year-old looked up into the face of a heavily bearded warrior who stood in front of him, also wearing a yellow turban, but it was ornamented with a large, gold broach like a shield with the letter D in its center. His blue uniform differed from the uniform of the man who had saved him in that it was covered with badges and bars and epaulettes and a broad, saffron sash that ran from his left shoulder across his barrel chest and to his right hip.

"My little son of India, listen to me," said the warrior. "I am the Rajah Agnimukha Dakkar, the King of Bundlekund. Listen to me. Listen. You are safe now. No one will harm you. You are not alone. You will come and live at my house, and eat my food. Do you understand?"

Something *exploded* in the ruins of the burning house, and the little boy jerked instinctively, beginning to turn to face his home. The hands of the Royal Guard on his shoulders stopped him, but he could still hear walls collapsing.

"He is the only one alive," said the guard to the warrior.

"What?!" said the boy.

"Well done," said the warrior, and picked the boy up. "It is a shame we didn't get here...in time."

Sobbing, the little one buried his face in the Rajah's salt-and-pepper beard against the monarch's barrel chest. Agnimukha wrapped him in his arms and patted his back with his dirty, blood-stained right hand. Then, after the boy's sobs began to diminished somewhat from emotional and physical exhaustion, the Rajah knelt, holding the boy back with a beefy hand by each of his shoulders to study his face.

"Let it out, my son," he said with a peace startling amidst the stench and noise and chaos. "Your tears are human and, therefore, not shameful. I would cry myself if I were in your place. Tell me, now. What is your name?"

It took a moment for the seven-year old to choke back his tears enough to whisper, "Indra."

"Because of the shameful horrors you have seen here, Indra, your life will change forever and you will never forget this day. But it is supremely important that you also remember something else as well. What was done here today *was* outrageously wrong. Neither my Gods nor your God condone what terrible things these narrow-minded, bigoted, foolish people did to your town, your church, your family. But today, you will, you *must*, make a choice that will determine the course of your life from this moment forward."

The boy wiped the tears from his cheeks and tried to listen. As he spoke, Agnimukha Dakkar fought to control his own emotions at what was behind the boy; two horrors driven like stakes into the ground on either side of the crumbling main entrance to what was now the blazing inferno of the little home church. The left, crude, wooden cross bore the bloody, crucified corpse of Indra's mother; the right, the corpse of his father.

"Today, you can choose to waste the rest of your life hating and seeking revenge on these murdering fools. You might even find and kill them someday. If you do so, you will become no better than them. Are you listening? Do you understand?"

Indra Singh nodded.

"Or you can choose what your mother and father chose; to forgive and bring love, and life, and healing to the world."

Agnimukha smiled.

"Now. We are going home. I have a new baby boy that needs a new big brother."

February, 1836. Bundlekund, India.

"Gentlemen, check your powder," said the Rajah Agnimukha Dakkar as he checked his own musket. "Today, we will either kill or be killed."

The Rajah stood with four other highly animated men and five thoroughbred horses on a landscaped clearing that abruptly ended in jungle not ten feet in front of his hunting party. That company was dressed in sturdy clothes designed by the Rajah; beige, double-breasted hunting jackets with an outer flap that ran diagonally from their right shoulders to the left side of their waists that was fastened up with pearl buttons. The tails of those jackets ended just above their knees. A black leather belt over the jacket at the waist sported a long, serrated knife sheathed on the left hip, and a single-shot pistol holstered on the right hip. The breeches below ended in heavy, leather boots, and jacket and breeches were of heavy, uncomfortable, hot broadcloth that, nevertheless, afforded some protection from the stings and bites of the swarms of insects in the jungle, and the thorns and brambles that pestered and tore at men. None of them cared a whit for comfort. Their nerves were in an heightened state of sensitivity and every thought was focused on the exhilaration of the hunt.

Four of the men wore beige turbans; the fifth was young, raven-haired, and bareheaded, and he, alone, bore the mark of caste on his forehead. Four of them carried muskets with the casual familiarity born of long experience; the fifth fisted his musket as if he were carrying a live, poisonous cobra. That fifth man was the eighteen-year-old Prince of Bundlekund, Rajesh Dakkar, recently returned from years spent at European universities.

"Rajesh," said Agnimukha as he glanced first at his son and then over his left shoulder at his palace three hundreds yards behind him. "Raj, what are you waiting for, an engraved gold invitation?"

Behind him, the Rajah's splendid palace stood in the center of a huge circle cleared of jungle trees and underbrush by two hundred hands, all in service to Agnimukha Dakkar. The jungle that surrounded the lawn was now constantly restrained by fifty gardeners.

The opulent, three-tiered, sandstone mansion was the center of the government of the Indian province. It was built with thirty-five bedrooms and ten bathrooms, and was also home for the Rajah, his wife, and his son. They shared seven dens, three libraries filled with rare manuscripts, and a grand ballroom, and the palace was furnished with innumerable rugs, paintings, tapestries, and well-stocked pantries as a testament to Agnimukha's power, wealth, and prestige. A wide, graveled road ran out of the jungle to the palace, lined on both sides with manicured trees, and a number of carriages of various sizes were parked before its massive entrance. Behind the palace was a small zoo because the Rajah preferred to capture rather than slay India's animals. Today, however, of necessity, would be an exception. A tiger must die.

Rajesh Dakkar nervously cleared his throat to interrupt his father's train of thought.

"I expected a more traditional celebration for my eighteenth birthday, father," he said, testing the balance of his musket by slightly swinging it up and down in small semi-circles in his right hand. "Considering my return after six years of study in Europe, where are my cake, the food, party favors and my extravagant presents? Where are my many friends? And why, oh why, must we hunt a tiger today of all days?"

"You have no friends," said the Rajah stroking his long, white beard with his right hand. "Nor do I. What we do have, due to our high position in Bundlekund, is a too-large collection of political and business associates who only want what we have, not friendship. We have cousins and uncles and aunts who share their covetousness and their lack of interest in us as human beings. And I have a wife, and you a mother, who loves us."

"And the tiger hunt on by eighteenth birthday? You know I hate bloodshed and have no interest in this."

"Too much talk, my son. We are here today to learn some lessons that can not be learned in a classroom or a laboratory. *Your* first lesson is that, for a genius who claims to know everything, *you* apparently *don't* have all the answers. Our window of opportunity will soon close, and the time for talk is done. Gentleman..." the Rajah began, only to again be interrupted by his son.

"Window?" said Rajesh, looking longingly back at the palace where he had carried out countless scientific experiments among a labyrinth of beakers, burners, alcohol lamps, flasks, test tubes, ring stands, stoppers, glass and rubber tubing, separation funnels, and other equipment of his own design, clockworks and chemicals from around the world, all staged in its elaborate basement. "You act as if the tiger was waiting for us with his friends the leopard, the elephant, and the monkey, at a table set with china for tea and a mechanical clock with an alarm."

"This answer and no more," said his father, frowning. "The time for talk is done, Raj. I earlier stationed a line of my best and most trusted men in the limbs of trees in the jungle. That line leads to a clearing in which I have placed a live doe staked to the ground by a length of rope and an open bucket of relatively fresh chicken's blood..."

"That's outrageous!" interrupted Rajesh, taking a step back from his father. "I can't believe..."

"Hush. That line of men relayed the news of the appearance of that tiger to a runner that carried the news to me at the palace. Everything for the hunt had been prepared in advance, and our fellow hunters were ready at the beat of a heart. It will not take that man-eating jungle cat three-quarters of an hour, if that, to slaughter that doe, fill its stomach and slink back into the jungle. We have but fifteen minutes left to kill the beast.

"Gentlemen!" he concluded as he turned from his son, and, waving his fellow hunters into action with the wave of his arm, barked, "Now!" And with no further word, he and his four fellows melted into the jungle.

They made no attempt to hide the noise of their movements, but still made little of it as they cautiously fanned out at approximately an arms length from one another in a relatively straight line. In the few moments that it took to leave the manicured lawn of the palace and travel through the jungle to the edge of the much smaller clearing with its staked prey, Rajesh glanced more than once at the father he had not seen in years who had given him every opportunity to experience life to its fullest, and had filled every need of his life. The man that was his father and Rajah was powerfully built, with a ruddy face, a white mane of hair beneath his turban, a paunch from too much rich food and drink, and a confidence that can be born only of power and long success. He was not a man to be questioned, so Rajesh forged ahead without further comment.

The intrusion of the hunters and the initial snarl of the tiger took all of ten eternal seconds. The hunters broke out of the forest at the edge of the clearing in the jungle almost as one. The tiger's huge orange and white head jerked up as their muskets were raised to their shoulders. There was no fear in the slanted, green pupils of its eyes, and a wealth of blood matted the hair around its jaws. Beneath its head lay the half eaten red mush of a shredded stomach of the doe, quite dead.

A dollop of slobber mixed with blood dripped from its jaws and ivory teeth to fall into the bloody wound in the doe. The tiger's mottled, long forelegs lay flat on the ground before the doe's belly, and its white hindquarters patched with orange were raised above the height of its head and shoulders and were swaying back and forth *as if* the great meat-eater kneaded the ground. It was not. The tiger snarled again and growled with a sound like a ratcheting tool, then roared. It less time than it took the hunters to draw a breathe, it leapt.

Dakkar awkwardly raised his musket to his right shoulder and fired it. The sound of the shot was absorbed by the heavy foliage of the thick jungle behind him. The kick of the musket painfully jerked the right side of his body back.

The musket ball struck the tiger a glancing blow on its left shoulder.

Thrown back slightly to its left side by the ball's impact, the tiger stopped, glanced at its wound, and then turned eyes burning with the fires of hell back to Dakkar. Dakkar lowered his musket and his hand instinctively fell to the knife sheathed on his hip.

Before Rajesh could draw that blade, Agnimukha, his musket firmly at his shoulder, took one step forwarded and fired as the tiger roared and leapt a second time.

The musket ball stuck the tiger just above and left of its left eye, slamming its head back on its neck. In reflex, its orange and white head snapped back to face the Rajah and Rajesh and the three hunters with muskets leveled at the rampaging beast. The tiger's jaw fell slack; its tongue lolling out of the left side of its mouth, and then the great carnivore fell with a sickening thud on its left flank to the ground, convulsing in the first throes of death.

Another eternity of seconds crawled by before anything human or beast moved.

"Gentlemen, assure our victory," said Agnimukha to his three hired musketeers who, as one, fired their own already raised weapons. The tiger's magnificent body jerked once, twice, and a third from the impact of the balls. Then the bloody, bullet-riddled tiger took a final breath, shuddered and lay still not three yards from Agnimukha, Rajesh, and the hunters who were now lowering their spent muskets. Agnimukha Dakkar looked at his son to gauge his emotional state as Rajesh looked at the tiger, more bewildered and detached from the ugly reality of the moment than frightened or distressed. Then the Rajah moved to the carcass and kicked it once in the neck. The tiger's massive head flopped back a bit and then forward a bit, but the man-eating beast was dead.

"Now, for the lesson, my son," said Agnimukha, looking up from the corpse. "The tiger is amoral, Rajesh. It does not kill out of envy or jealousy or greed. It kills to eat. You, however, have at least a vestige of morality hidden somewhere beneath your amazing intellect, so you should know that this tiger was killed because we know, with certainly, that it has killed and eaten at least one child in a nearby village. We suspect more than one, and it certainly would have killed again, once tasting human blood. Therefore, it had to die.

"There are no saints on any battlefield, Raj. Saints don't survive battles. There are no saints here, right now. Not you. Not me. Not my men. So as you choose the men you need for this harebrained expedition you are putting together to find only the gods know what, and although I don't quite understand every aspect of what you propose to do, I do know this. To kill the tiger, I hired expert marksmen, not saints. I needed men who don't miss targets. You, in your turn, need men with the particular skills needed to accomplish your mission. To choose these men on any other basis would be the height of folly .

"Indra Singh can save their souls afterwards."

Chapter Two

April, 1836

The door *bang* slammed open against the right wall in which it was set. "There he is!" barked the bullfrog voice of the outraged, flaccid father standing in his olive green nightclothes in the threshold of the door to his daughter's opulent bedroom. "Kill him!"

Clutching a yellow, silk sheet to her breast to hide her nakedness, his young daughter, whose beauty put Helen of Troy to shame, leapt out of her huge, overstuffed bed. In the instant that the sheet was snatched away, her lover, dressed only in white underpants, threw his lean, powerful legs over the side of the mattress onto the floor next to where his boots stood at the foot of a lit brazier.

He said, "Zut!"

That source of the bedroom's light stood on an elaborate stand by the bed's mahogany headboard where his shirt, pants and scabbard were draped. He snatched his unsheathed foil from where it leaned against the wall next to the brazier as the enraged and indignant father stomped into the bedroom. Three men dressed in imitation of Napoleon's army and armed with foils and short swords, stepped in after him, their foils drawn.

The tall, athletic man in his underpants stood up, straight and unafraid.

"Hello," he said as he stroked the right side of his thin black mustache with the manicured index finger of his left hand. "May I introduce myself? I am Andrew Legrand, the greatest swordsman in all of France. And too modest to mention, the greatest lover as well."

"My cherie," he addressed his lover as the bullfrog stepped to one side to allow his personal henchmen to stride in three steps to the bed. "It appears we have unexpected guests."

The veins in his face flushed with blood lust, and pointing a fat finger at his daughter's lover, the bullfrog again croaked, "Kill him!"

"I am Andrew Legrand..."

"If it pleases you," said Andrew, "not this night." So saying, he tipped over the golden brazier on its filigreed, golden legs.

His lover yelped and turned her tear-stained face to the rich, velvet embroidered wallpaper of her boudoir.

"Oh, oh, oh," said the green mottled bullfrog and danced on tiptoes to the wall furthest from the searing coals fanning across the lushly carpeted floor.

The first mistake his guards made was to join in the dance.

Andrew hopped backwards onto the mattress as the toad cried out, "The carpet is on fire!"

The Frenchman bounced up, drawing his knees to his chest, and kicked both guards in the face. They stumbled back several steps, dropping their foils, then fell to the floor like clubbed bulls, clutching broken noses with their gloved hands and moaning.

Andrew leapt over the writhing bodies of the felled duo, and, in two bounds, faced the father of his lover. In a breath, the raiser-sharp tip of his foil was at the throat of the bullfrog who slowly lowered himself to his fat knees, his hands clutched together in silent prayer.

"Have no fear, my friend. The wages of *my* sin," grinned the Frenchman, "is not *your* death," and, turning, he ran back to the bed, snatched up his shirt and pants, and headed for the open bedroom door. Reaching its threshold, he paused and bowed slightly at the waist.

"Mademoiselle," he said, "Parting is such sweet sorrow. Au revoir."

Andrew Legrand glanced quickly left and then right down the elaborately carpeted, decorated, and furnished hallway leading from the bedroom. As he heard the toad screaming the alarm behind him, he saw three heavily armed men loping down the hall towards him from his right side. They were no more than ten feet away.

"Gentlemen," he grinned, "goodbye," and stepped into the hall.

Without hesitation and with supreme confidence, the Frenchman began to run down the hallway to his left, passing cabinets filled with treasures, grand, overstuffed chairs, and small cherry-wood tables standing against wall-papered walls hung with oil paintings, framed mirrors, and rich tapestries.

Pausing only a second in mid-flight, he grabbed the edge of a cherry-wood cabinet filled with an eclectic collection of porcelain, ceramic, china, and wooden figures of cats and toppled it *crash* to the floor as he passed it.

The first of the three guards pursuing the Frenchman tried in vain to sidestep the cabinet, but struck it hard. His feet failing to find footing among the puzzle of cats scattered on the floor, he managed to yell one profanity and then fell on his face. Glancing over his shoulder as he ran, Andrew laughed heartily.

The second and then third of the guards fell over the first and then themselves in a chaos of arms and legs and foils and curses as Andrew neared the end of the hallway and a door to his left side. With no other good choice, the swordsman threw open the door that struck the wall in which it was set with a loud bang as he looked through its threshold and down into a descending stairway.

"Sacre blue!' he said to himself, "All this for one night of stolen kisses?"

He saw two more armed guards at the foot of the stairs ascending with cautious glances. Those glances turned to snarls as they saw Andrew above them, and one raised his fist and shook it.

Since Andrew could not go back without a heightened chance of death, the Frenchman leapt up on the stair's banister as if straddling a horse.

"Hello!" he cried out at the guards climbing the stairs as he began to slide down the banister, flourishing his foil.

"Goodbye!" he chortled as he passed them, spanking them one time with his foil.

In the same instance, and almost as one, both guards began to turn, trying to snatch the Frenchman who had already slid past them to the bottom of the banister, jumped off, and was running across the landing to its open doorway.

His farewell was met with curses and shaken fists.

Andrew stepped through the door into another hall divided by a partial wall the height of his shoulders from a second, parallel hallway. Both passageways ended several feet shy and to his right of a large window and to his left in four armed men approaching with resolve written on their sober faces.

His decision made for him; Andrew jumped into the hall, turned to his right, and began to run next to the dividing wall and towards the window. With a united shout, the armed guards leapt into heated pursuit, and, at the same instance, the left shoulder, left arm, and head of a man wearing a red beret bobbed up behind them on the opposite side of the dividing wall in seeming pursuit of the guards. In his balled, gloved fist was a black, leather blackjack.

As the six men lopped down the hallway, the blackjack struck the head of the guard at the rear of the runners who, unseen by his fellows, collapsed like a dead weight to the floor. The man in the red beret kissed the blackjack and smiled.

Again, the blackjack came down on the head of the guard at the rear of the runners who also collapsed to the floor, striking the shoulder of the guard ahead of him in his fall.

The third guard looked over his shoulder as he ran. The blackjack broke his nose.

Seconds away from the window, Andrew glanced back over his shoulder to see the last remaining guard collapse on the floor as the blackjack struck him on the back of his head like a hammer, and the man in the red beret laughed and waved a greeting to the Frenchman.

Incredulous, Andrew stumbled to a stop at the window, his foil raised in defense. He scratched his head with his free hand, sending his shirt and pants sliding up to his triceps, as he took inventory of the line of unconscious men littering the floor. Incredulity turned to astonishment as his unknown savior stepped from behind the dividing wall.

He whispered, "What is this!"

The man in the red beret with the blackjack was a dwarf sitting on the shoulders of a perhaps seventeen or eighteen year old man of Indian descent with the red mark of caste on his forehead.

"Who..?" Andrew began to speak.

"No time," said the Indian. He lowered himself to his knees and the dwarf jumped off his shoulders. "More guards are on the way. Open the window."

"Why!?!"

"Open the window!" commanded the young Indian.

"Oui." Andrew threw open the window.

The Indian leaned out of it, waved his gloved hands, and then withdrew himself.

"Stand away from the window," he added as he and the dwarf pressed themselves against the wall. "Now!"

"You bet," Andrew said and moved to one side.

There was a terrific, audible *whoosh* of air from somewhere below them.

A grapple on the end of a line hurtled through the window, fell *thud* several feet into the hallway onto the floor, and was then drawn back until its tines caught the window sill.

"It is beyond belief," Andrew whispered as he returned to the window and looked down to a small boat on the river that ran next to the bullfrog's mansion.

Another Indian, bald headed and very large, was seated next to what looked like a small, thin cannon in the boat. The line attached to the grapple ran to the mouth of the cannon.

"As they says in America, yahoo!"

"Wrap your hands in your shirt, grab the line, and slide down," said the younger Indian, smiling with the self-confidence born of youth.

"I think the frog-eater is an idiot," said the dwarf.

"Your wish, my Indian friend," said the Frenchman, "is my command."

"Now I *know* he is a moron."

Andrew wrapped his hands in his shirt.

Chapter Three

Ten years after the rare and joyous birth of Aiguo Chop and his twin brother, Bohai, in the summer of 1810, Daoguang became the eighth Emperor of the Manchu Qing dynasty and the sixth Qing Emperor to rule over China. The twins were born on the edge of a tiny village about fifteen miles northeast of the palace of the Emperor to poor parents who lived hand-to-mouth lives barely earning enough to feed themselves. But Aiguo and Bohai, who lived in rags and some days ate nothing but air and tearful promises knew nothing else and were happy. By the time they were seven years old, their days were spent working at menial jobs around the village or in playing at being fierce warriors. Their weapons were imitations of the cleavers their father used to butcher livestock; toy cleavers carved out of wood. By time they were fifteen years old, Aiguo and Bohai could drop a bird in mid-flight at one hundred feet with their father's real cleavers.

The Emperor Daoguang's hedonism and vanity had no limits, and his lust for power was unparalleled. He adorned himself, his entourage, his family, and his palace in shameless luxury at the expense of his own poverty stricken people. Diamonds were his teardrops and his underclothes were silk. Beneath his clothing, his was a slobber of flesh. It was therefore not surprising that, beginning in 1820, Daoguang's thirty year reign would be marred by disaster and rebellion among his subjects, first by the bloody First Opium War, and then by the equal butchery of the Taiping Rebellion that nearly brought down his rule. By 1835, when Aiguo and Bohai were twenty six years old, and at the end of his first decade as the decadent Emperor of the largest nation on earth, the Emperor's dynasty began to slowly fall apart.

Large parts of his empire were on the verge of anarchy as regional warlords raised their own armies to conquer and pillage their neighbors, famine born of drought threatened death and madness to half of his people, murderers and highwaymen where as common as dust and foreign nations were rattling bloody swords. It seemed that China was falling apart like an assembled puzzle dashed against a wall. It was then that Daoguang sent out his most trusted and feared General Jiang with a large contingency of the most ruthless warriors in China to destroy those who threatened his dominance.

It was a month after Jiang's deployment that Daoguang's most beloved of daughters, the beautiful and headstrong Princess Duanmin, set her chin against her father and secretly disguised herself, one trusted attendant, and one palace guard as commoners to visit a beloved cousin who lived thirty miles to the north of Daoguang's heavily guarded Imperial Palace. She had lived a sheltered life, so Duanmin hired a shoddy carriage with four poorly used horses, dressed her attendant as a peasant and the palace guard as her driver, and defied her father in the misguided belief that only a fool would try to rob a peasant.

When her carriage had traveled but five miles into the countryside, four men frothing at their mouths like savage, starved orangutans sprang from behind the trees on a small embankment and skidded down its slope, screaming and brandishing clubs spiked with iron nails, one musket, and two polished butcher's cleavers. Before the driver could even whip his horses into a gallop, the highway men were upon them.

"Drop the reins! Get down and step away from the carriage!" yelled Enlai, the tallest of the highwaymen, in the native language of the Chinese. So saying, he waved the only musket owned by the four destitute thieves at the driver. Indignant, and at the worst possible moment, Duanmin stuck her her out of one of the carriage's window.

"*Driver*, why did you stop..." she began, but her final word fell apart when she saw Enlai and his three dirty, emancipated highwaymen.

The driver gripped the sheathed sword upon which he sat to hide it and stood up.

"I will die before I do either!" he sneered.

"As you wish," responded Enlai, and *blam* shot him through the heart. His body toppled, lifeless, to the ground at Enlai's dirty, sandaled feet. Since he had spent the only bullet they owned, Enlai tossed the musket away.

Duanmin's head bobbed back into the carriage.

"Are you out of your mind!" Aiguo demanded of his fellow thug. "We agreed there would be *no* killing!"

Enlai ignored Aiguo, turned to Hulin, and barked, "Get up there and free those horses!"

Hulin said, "But I don't know anything…"

"Get up there!" screamed his fellow thief. "Our people are starving! Free those horses!"

Bohai stepped up to Enlai, his hand on the cleaver tucked under his twisted, cloth belt, and said, "If we steal their horses, someone else is sure to kill two stranded women on this lonely road."

"You are right," said Enlai as Hulin clumsily tried to mount the carriage to the driver's seat. "You!" he shouted, turning from Bohai to the coach. "You in the coach. Get out here now!"

Aiguo had joined his twin, his hand on his cleaver as well, as the door to the coach opened and Duanmin and her companion, who was sobbing, left their seats inside.

"We agreed to steal horses and money," said Aiguo, "and anything we could find to feed our people left in the village after it was ravaged by that swarm of human locusts, Enlai. That and nothing more. You have already broken our agreement. You will not break it again."

"Really?" said Enlai as he watched the two women descend the carriage to the ground. "You two, throw whatever you have of value on the ground. Now!"

"We have nothing of value," lied Duanmin as she and her attendant stood, trembling, before the four thieves.

"You have one thing," said Enlai. "Your eyes. With those pretty eyes, you could identify us. So those pretty eyes must close forever." And, so saying, he raised his club and took a step towards the women who cringed back against the coach.

The honed edge of Aiguo's cleaver was at Enlai's throat before he could swallow.

"Drop the club, Enlai," he snarled as he brother snatched his cleaver from his belt as well. "Drop it, or I will gut you like a pig! Get off the carriage, Hulin. Brother, get his club."

Enlai dropped his club.

"What you *will* do," continued Aiguo, "is take two horses back to our village to feed the starving. The remaining horses will be left to carry these women back home. Can you ride, ladies?"

Duanmin nodded her affirmation.

"You will take the horses, Enlai, and we will follow after you shortly. When we all arrive back home, I will let the village decide your punishment. But be certain that any attempt to do other than what I have said will end with my cleaver in your skull."

Hulin, who was a coward, joined Enlai who was shaking with rage and shame as he released the two lead horses from the carriage. Together, they began to steer the horses up onto the slope and into the stand of trees by the side of the dirt road.

Duanmin studied the twins who each wore a brown top-knot tied with a dirty, blue ribbon on the back third of their otherwide bald heads, ragged and filthy off-white linen undershirts that fell to mid-thigh beneath their waist-long tattered, yellow vests, and sandaled feet.

"You have saved us," she said. "You will be richly rewarded."

Aiguo looked at her common clothes, undressed hair, and lack of adornment as she stood before the battered carriage with its two well-worn horses, and said, "You owe us nothing. Our faith in Buddha forbids the taking of life; of any human life."

"Your faith and courage has saved you and your village forever after," said Duanmin. "I am the Princess Duanmin."

Scrubbed clean, well-feed for six months, and dressed in the finest military uniforms, Aiguo and Bohai Chop rigidly stood on either side of the fabulous golden throne of Emperor Daoguang in the opulent interior courtroom of the eighth Emperor of the Manchu Qing dynasty and the sixth Qing Emperor to rule over China. Their cleavers at their hips were sheathed for the first time in their lives in oiled, pig-skin holsters, and each held a spear whose butt rested by the heel of their left feet. The Emperor wore multi-layered robes of the rarest of silks studded with tiny emeralds and diamonds, a gold crown topped his powered hair, and diamond rings on each of his visible fingers. The Royal Sculptor knelt next to a court guard at the foot of the stairs that led to the throne.

The reward the twins had won was their positions as the Emperor's personal bodyguards, and the promise that their mother, sisters, friends, and neighbors in their ravaged village were clothed, well fed, and safe in an otherwise chaotic world. As Duoguang's bodyguards, they were attendant to the Emperor during every waking moment of every day, and had access to almost every room in the Imperial Palace. When the Emperor learned of and then saw their amazing prowess with the cleaver, they also were required to exhibit their unsurpassed agility with the deadly blades to the elite of China and visiting dignitaries at Duoguang's slightest whim.

The price that came with the reward was high. So that there could never be a chance that court secrets would be even accidentally passed on to undeserving ears, the Emperor had cut out their tongues.

"Rise up," Duoguang commanded of his sculptor. As was customary,

Aiguo and Bohai struck the floor with the butt of their spears for added emphasis. "Tomorrow we will unveil your masterpiece, the statue of your Emperor, in this very court and before all of the elite of China. I anticipate awe and applause. Disappointment, however, will lead to your death. Now, leave me."

Duoguang looked at the guard at the foot of the stairs and said, "Bring in General Jiang."

As the guard left to fetch the General, Duoguang turned first to Aiguo and then to Bohai.

"Tomorrow, you each will also be dressed in the finest that my Royal clothiers can produce."

Aiguo and then Bohai nodded and smiled.

General Jiang and a handful of his highest officers marched down the center of the court, heavily armed and in full military regalia, and presented themselves with elaborate bows to their Emperor. After his formal greeting, Jiang reported with great pride that it had been necessary to severely punish several villages in the past months that had continued to resist the Emperor's rule by killing every one in each hovel, and then named the villages one by one.

The third village named had been where Aiguo and Bohai's mother and three sisters had lived.

The attentive might have noticed the blood drain from Aiguo and Bohai's faces, and saw the blue veins rise on the back of their hands as they clenched their spears, and beneath the congratulations of the Emperor, heard the grinding of their teeth.

In the dead silence of night, Emperor Duoguang awoke in bed with Aiguo's cleaver at his throat.

In the morning, one hundred and fifty of China's aristocracy had crowded in the gilded court. Among these men and women were the high bred, the politically and economically influential, the brilliant, the wealthy, and the gifted of the nation. The total value of their rings and bracelets, tiaras, medals, necklaces, earrings and rich clothing surpassed the total income of the remainder of China. A low murmur of anticipation and the whispered question, "where's the Emperor?" filled the air.

Heavily armed soldiers lined the walls of the court, and General Jiang stood uneasily next to an eight foot tall cubicle constructed from brass poles and velvet curtains in front of Duoguang's throne. He continuously looked to his right and left as he held a braided cord that, when pulled, would drop the curtains to the floor, revealing the magnificent statue of the Emperor of China.

After long moments, Jiang shrugged his shoulders, thanked the crowd for attending, excused the Emperor's absence due to an emergency that demanded his attention, and pulled the cord.

The curtain fell in folds to the floor.

As one, the crowd gasped. A first and then a second woman screamed. There was a movement, a tide of outraged human flesh trying and failing to push its way through the crowd and out of the court.

The blood drained from Jiang's face, and he leapt in front of the Emperor's statue.

Tied to the seven-and-a-half foot tall statue of Duoguang, gagged and with his head lowered and turned to his left side, was the sagging, dissipated body of the naked Emperor, struggling not only against the ropes that bound him to the statue, but in a vain attempt to hide his utter humiliation. But he could not raise his pudgy, bound hands to bury his face in them.

A titter ran through his subjects that grew and spread and became an uproarious laughter that overwhelmed the Emperor's sobs.

Chapter Four

May, 1836.

Despite his height, Indra Singh had threaded half way through the maze of desks piled high with scientific equipment in Rajesh Dakkar's laboratory before he caught sight of the Prince of Bundlekund hunched over a large desk at the back of his rented home base in Palestine.

"Rajesh!" he called out, but received no answer. Shrugging his shoulders, he placed the palm of his right hand on the edge of the massive table and paused for a moment. On the table, among a clutter of scientific apparatus, sat a very small furnace with a glowing fire in it, and above the fire, two glass crucibles connected by a glass tube. One of these crucibles was nearly full of melted lead. The other crucible held some unidentifiable liquid that was slowly dissipating in a vapor. The vapor stank. Singh pinched his nostrils with the fingers of his left hand, shook his head in disapproval, and then continued down the maze.

Several minutes later, Indra stopped behind Rajesh who was still completely absorbed in what was spread out of the surface of the desk before him, a very large and intricate blueprint drawn by hand in India ink.

"My Lord..." Singh began.

Rajesh jerked upright. "What?" He turned with a sincere expression of surprise and momentary confusion when he saw his tutor. He ran a hair through his disheveled, raven black hair. "Indra, what are you doing here?"

"My job. What on earth," he said, pointing at the blueprint, "is that?"

Rajnesh smiled and turned back to his diagram to trace one of its lines with the index finger of his right hand. "She's a 152 ton brig, Singh, and all mine. See here on the side? That's the vent for the release of steam."

"Steam, my Lord?"

"I'm sure I've asked you a thousand times not to call me 'Lord'. Could you do that for me? Yes, steam. When she isn't driven by the wind, the Nautilus will be driven across the Mediterranean by steam. She was built under my direction, is fully outfitted, and waits for us and my Black Knights on the coast. Isn't she a beauty?"

"A beauty, indeed," said Singh, swabbing his bald pate from front to back with his right hand. "What are Black Knights?"

"Oh, the Black Knights is my little pet name for the men who will form my expedition."

"And may I finally be privy to just what your expedition will seek?"

"That," said Rajesh, "will have to remain my secret until the moment is right, Indra, and this is not that moment. Now, my nosy friend, what are you doing here?"

"There are two men from China who wish an audience with you, Rajesh."

"She is called the 'Nautilus', Indra," said Rajesh.

"I know, my Prince. You've told me her name fifty times. There are two men from China who wish to talk to you, Rajesh."

"China? They have traveled far. Do they have names, or is this a game of puzzles?"

"They have traveled far and long. They told me they have searched for themselves for almost a year across Europe until they found themselves... here. As for names, I don't know. They can't speak."

"Then how do you they traveled for a year, Indra. Can you read minds?"

"They can write."

So saying, Indra handed Rajesh a piece of folded paper.

"Their names are written here, and they want to join a fool's expedition."

Rajesh took the paper, unfolded it, and read what was written there.

"And they can't say a single word?" he asked, raising an eyebrow.

"Well, not exactly. One of them said something like 'maziqlda.'"

Chapter Five

September, 1836.

Deep in the angry, red bowels of the massive cavern beneath the ancient Egyptian city of Alexandria, water churned and rushed through a jointed copper pipe that was bolted into the iron side of a huge, gurgling boiler that huffed and clanked and huffed again. Sweating, grunting, and cursing, heavily muscled men stripped to their waists and chained by iron bands on their ankles to iron rings in the floor shoved shovels into a huge mound of black coal, lifted their burdens, and tossed them into the fiery jaws of the boiler's hungry, boiling belly. They and countless men before them had been coerced into this back-breaking labor since Alexandria was seized from the Byzantine Empire in bloody battle by the Arabian forces of the Rashidun Caliphate in the middle of the 7th century AD.

The water inside the boiler boiled and hissed into steam that forced internal pistons up and down and up and down and pumped it into the attached copper pipe. That pipe became two smaller tubes at its first exterior joint that disappeared into the stone walls of the cavern, then two became four, then six, screaming up and up and up through an ever growing web of small, red-hot copper pipes that honeycombed the myriad tunnels of the massive cave like human veins.

The steam hissed and screamed through substations hidden behind the cavern walls to their innumerable final destinations, throwing interconnected gears on their way, then passing on, lifting levers that opened or shut values that lifted or set, moved or stopped innumerable hidden mechanisms. It had been built with an incredibly ancient and complex knowledge of hydraulics that had been lost to the world above for centuries.

An uncalloused hand touched an almost invisible stud in the plastered wall of the tunnel, and one of those unnumbered copper veins opened a vent that threw a switch that jerked interlocking iron gears into motion. Protesting a pressure not to be denied, a stone slab door slowly grumbled and rose from its niched threshold in the floor.

"Mother of God, that's the fourth time a door has opened by itself," said

Father Robert Allen who stood just behind the opening slab, "and I'm still not used to it!"

There was no acknowledgment of the middle-aged priest's words from the hooded man who had pushed the stud. Instead, his waved arm was a silent invitation for the priest to pass through the opened portal ahead of him. The excited priest needed no added incentive.

Father Allen stepped across the threshold, noting that another rough slab was blocking the corridor not twenty feet in front of him, creating another dead end in what had become so complex a maze of tunnels that the priest had lost all sense of time, depth, or direction. The thought flashed through his mind that he was hopelessly lost with no hope of find his way out of the subterranean Library of Alexandria that had been concealed under the city since the the Arabic conquest of Egypt. The Catholic priest shrugged his shoulders in surrender to his vulnerability; his gesture was not imitated by the two cowled figures holding smoldering torches immediately behind him..

The Jesuit stopped, reached out, and touched the cavern wall with his gloved left hand.

"I still can't believe I'm actually here," Father Allen said to the cowled men a foot or so behind him and at his right and left sides. His words echoed faintly in the otherwise eerie silence.

"Of course, we've had our suspicions, and our knowledge about you Soters and the priceless knowledge and treasures of antiquity you have protected these countless centuries is incomplete, but to actually be *walking down this passageway*...I am the most blessed of men.

"This tunnel has been enlarged and improved by human hands," the Jesuit priest noted as he lay the index finger of his right hand on the side of his nose. "Just like the others. How many years of thankless toil and ruined backs did that require?"

Father Allen smiled, trying to be pleasant, and dropped his left hand and nervously wiped it on his off-white canvas shirt already stained with sweat at both armpits and around his collarbone. The tiny cross that hung from a chain around his neck and lay against his collarbone was gold.

Neither of the hooded figures said a word. Their faces and, therefore, their expressions and emotions, were hidden by their cowls and the outre dancing shadows thrown by the low burning torches embedded in the chiseled walls and the braziers standing at irregular intervals in the passageway. Their bodies and their body language was hidden by the folds of long-sleeved, grey robes with bands of embroidered, blue, Egyptian cartouches at their wrist and hemlines. Neither their silence nor the close, damp air in the tunnel did anything to bolster Father Allen's courage, nor dampen his resolve.

"Well, I guess it doesn't matter," he added as he continued his journey down the corridor. "I didn't expect to learn *everything* on my trip here. But I'm certain you can understand that the initial excitement and joy I felt when I received your map and letter has not abated one whit. It was the answer to years of fervent prayer and supplication. What's...?"

His words cut short; the priest had stopped abruptly before a deep niche cut from the cavern's stone wall on his right side and about five feet short of the blocked end of the corridor. A shudder ran through his body like an electric shock. Inside, a bleached skull five times larger than the head of any man he'd ever seen sat on a small, ivory pedestal also covered with arcane cartouches.

It had *one* jagged, gaping eye socket just above a now nonexistent nose.

Father Allen looked at the two robed figures standing behind him. Both seemed indifferent.

The hooded Soter to his left said, "We are here," and touched the wall to his right side. An unseen copper vein opened a vent that threw a switch that jerked interlocking iron gears into motion. The stone slab door grumbled and rose from its niched threshold.

Father Allen quickly took the three steps to the opened door and stopped. It did *not* open on another tunnel.

A fall of stairs before and below the priest spiraled at least twenty feet down to the floor of a vast cavern. The priest gasped and shuddered involuntarily with ecstasy. Its length and breath and organized chaos of shelving and niches and crates, outre statues and antediluvian artifacts, stretched in a vanishing perspective that exceeded the limits of his vision. An incalculable number of torches and braziers dimly lit a staggering wealth of archaic bound manuscripts, stacked loose pages of parchment and papyrus, scrolls, and metallic and stone tablets that filled those shelves. The smell of antiquity hung in the air like musk as the Jesuit tried and failed to mentally catalog Egyptian sarcophagi, Persian scepters, Babylonian torture devices, Assyrian fetishes, Grecian urns, Mesopotamian tapestry, the clay tablets of Ur, a bronze, Canaanite bas-relief of Baal, Sumeric and Chinese and African weaponry....

Breathless, Father Allen stood overwhelmed and uncharacteristically speechless for long moments before he whispered, "Sweet Mother of God. This is beyond all imagination!"

The Jesuit opened his arms in symbolic embrace as he looked first to his left side and then to his right side at his Stoic hooded guides. They did not speak. They did not move.

"This is almost beyond belief! Somewhere in those stacks are the lost books of Adam and Noah and Enoch, the original Gospel parchments, the missives of Thomas to the churches in India! This makes the Bibliotheca Apostolica Vaticana in Rome look like a school girl's library!"

His arms still spread wide in awe, the Jesuit stepped out onto the landing of the wide, stone steps that, cut from the walls of the cavern, led to the floor of the unbelievably huge chamber below him. Father Allen glanced up.

"What is that?" he asked because, his vision foreshortened by his position, the priest could not piece together in his mind's eye the two huge, oak beams—the smaller bolted and perpendicular to the larger at its lower third—that were attached flat to the wall above him with iron latches.

The two beams were wild with razor sharp iron spikes.

The hooded figure behind and to the Jesuit's left reached out and touched the cavern wall with his left hand; a tiny square of stone soundlessly sunk into its surface.

The Jesuit priest said, "We'll have to be careful. These stair are step," and took a step forward.

The iron gears hidden behind the wall jerked into motion. The priest heard a thin almost imperceptible whistle like steam escaping a tea pot. The latches on the beams sprang open.

Father Allen added, "They'll never believe this at the abbey."

Freed from their restraint, the crossed beams in the wall above the priest fell forward and down on pivots embedded in the wall in a long descending arc, its iron swivels protesting from long unoiled neglect, and swinging down...

thuck

...impaled Father Allen.

Father Allen said, "uuuck."

A thick, red pool gathered at the right sandal of the cowled man who stood left of where the priest hung with a hundred new, bloody mouths. The Soter pushed the cowl back from his face.

Mocking the priest in a sing song voice, he said, "What is that?

The Eye of Horus painted on Ptah's forehead did not blink.

"Why, the cross you must bear."

Chapter Six

He wore neither a blindfold nor a gag.

Every inch of Henny Lagle's seven feet stood straight and proud with the defiance and fearlessness of a hardened mercenary in front of the five man firing squad. His uniform was tattered and dirty; the seam at his left shoulder had been torn loose. His great mane of blond hair, although also dirty and in disarray, had been combed and re-combed and re-combed again with the only thing he possessed besides his uniform, his fingers. His walrus mustache had been cleaned as best he could with his own spit. The hands he had used to try to groom himself were now tied behind his back with hemp rope. He squinted against the hard light of the sun overhead

On the far left end of his soon to be executioners, each aiming a musket at Henny's chest, stood am almost equally tall man, evidentially muscular even beneath the long, grey robe he wore, his face hidden in the deep shadow cast by his cowl. His feet were sandaled; a hair belt circled his waist, and a large, wooden cross hung by a leather thong on his chest. His head was bowed.

Just moments ago as the Prussian and the cowled priest had walked down a long hallway to the courtyard of the prison, the priest had said, "No matter how many men you have killed, Jesus can still save you at this very moment."

Henny had answered, "I have done more than just *kill* men, Father."

"It doesn't matter," said the priest. "He can save you nevertheless."

"It mattered to them." Henny smiled. "Don't feel sorry for me, Father. It doesn't really matter that Jesus won't save me since I don't believe in him."

To the right side of the firing squad stood another soldier whose medals indicated higher rank holding a sword flat against his right thigh with his right hand. He wore a uniform identical to that worn by the men with muskets; none wore Henny's uniform.

He raised the sword and barked, "Fire!"

Like the chatter of exploding firecrackers, the muskets discharged.

Henny was jerked back hard *thup thup thup* by the impact of three bullets. Two bullets struck the wall behind him. He stumbled several steps backwards, struck the wall, and slid down its rough planks to sit, slumped, on the ground.

The leader of the death squad said, "Gentlemen...you are dismissed."

As the five executioners began to disperse, two men with a burlap stretcher appeared in the doorway behind them, sidestepped the gunmen as they approached, and then walked solemnly to Henny's body. The priest joined them at the corpse.

As the priest genuflected over the body and began to pray quietly, they lifted the Prussian's body with some effort onto the stretcher, then carried it to a waiting, one-mule wagon at the edge of the courtyard. The priest turned away as they slid the stretcher and its grisly burden onto the bed of the wagon. The driver of the cart did not look back from his seat as they covered the body with a tarp lying on the bed of the wagon.

Its driver snapped his whip over the mule hitched to it, and the wagon startled into a slow gait into the cobblestoned street before it.

The cart rolled and lumbered down the street with the urgency of drying paint, passing small shops and customers entering and leaving their doorways, and weaved its way past women, some with children skittish with restraint, and men milling about until the city slowly fell away behind them.

Twenty minutes outside the city, when the no longer cobblestoned road before him wound its way for a seeming eternity before him except for stands of trees on either side, the driver looked over his shoulder, ran a hand through his raven black hair, and pulled back on the reins to stop the mule.

"We're clear," he said.

Henny rose up in the bed of the wagon beneath the tarp, and tossed it to one side.

"I don't know how to thank you," he said, taking a deep breath and rubbing his chest with his beefy hands. "Even though they were blanks, they still hurt a little. What's next?"

"You can thank my mentor for switching the shells later, my friend. Next, we abandon this snail of a wagon," continued the driver as he dismounted from his seat, "for a much faster vehicle hidden in the stand of trees just to our left."

As the swarthy driver and the Prussian walked into the first cluster of trees, the driver said, "Maybe next time, you'll be a marksman for the *winning* side, eh, Mr. Lagle?"

"Yay. Next time. Just why did you bother with me?"

The driver said nothing as they penetrated the outermost cluster of trees and Henny stopped dead in his tracks.

"Godt in Himmel! What is that?"

The driver chuckled under his breath.

He walked to the side of a magnificent, oversized carriage where the hooded priest that had tried to give him his last rights stood with a hand on an opened door. All of its polished brass fittings and its mahogany slats seemed to tremble with pent up pressure, and was easily twice as large as any normal carriage the Prussian had ever seen. There was no horse to draw it and no driver's seat. A large, plate glass window had replaced that seat: the driver steered the vehicle from a space behind the window and in front of the lush passenger's compartment by what looked like a helmsman's wheel. The rubber rimmed wheels were also oversized and seemingly inflated, and two large vents on the left and right sides of the carriage were huffing clouds of smoke.

"That is my mentor, Indra Singh. My name is Rajesh Dakkar."

"No, no. Not the priest. The thing!"

"Indra is not actually a priest, Mr. Lagle. 'The thing' is a steam driven carriage, and my invention. It will easily do twenty miles an hour or slightly more with a full head of steam.

"And it is your ticket to adventure."

October, 1836.

Prince Rajesh Dakkar tottered fearlessly on the top spar of the central mast of his 152 ton brig, the Nautilus, a young god, a 19th century Adonis, muscular and perfectly proportioned, his bronze skin unblemished and vibrant with health. The ship's main sail was furled beneath his feet. The brig's massive steam engine lay unseen, pensive and asleep in the bottom hold of the stern.

In the exhilaration of youth, he threw his head back and laughed.

Energized and eager, Dakkar glanced to the port side of the Nautilus at the serene, blue-green waters of the Mediterranean and the distant orange and yellow sun sinking into the horizon. He glanced up at the otherwise cerulean blue sky spotted with white, harmless clouds that seemed to hang motionless above him. He took in a long, deep breath, relishing the tang of the brisk, salty air.

Rajesh's nose was aquiline, his grey eyes wide-set, and his skin was naturally swarthy even when not bronzed by the sun. He laughed again in selfless celebration of his physical strength and life with neither shame at his near-naked, eighteen year old body, nude except for a cotton breech clout, nor pride in his physical superiority to the dwarf and the giant far below him on deck.

The dwarf and the Frenchman below him did not share his self-evaluation.

Rajesh Dakkar shook his mane of raven black hair, and, unaware that he did so, touched the red dot of paste just above his eyes and on the center of his forehead with the index finger of his left hand. It was a Shudra "bindi", the lowest Hindu caste ordaining an Indian as a laborer, artisan or servant, and outrageously inappropriate for a Prince of India. His right hand gripped the mast of the brig, helping him maintain his balance against the gentle pitch of the Nautilus.

Rajesh said aloud to himself, "Not a breeze anywhere. If this continues, I'll have to fire-up my boiler at first dawn. Pity."

He looked down, took a second deep breath, and cupped a hand to the side of his mouth.

He shouted, "Heads up! The eagle flies!" and closed his eyes.

Olaf Templeton, the dwarf on the deck below, looked up from the padlock he had just jimmied open with a skeleton key and sneered at the sound of his captain's voice.

"'Eagle' my ass, eh, Andrew? Rajesh Dakkar is an idiot," he said, standing with his legs spread unnaturally far apart and flat-footed to hold his own balance on the brig's deck. Even in his black, whale-hide boots, the disgruntled dwarf only reached the waist of Andrew Legrand, the lanky Frenchman sitting on a green deck chair next to him. His face buried in an open book, Andrew grunted in response as if he were actually listening.

The dwarf shoved the lock and key in the front left pocket of his canvas jeans and again looked up at Dakkar balanced on the spar of the mast. His pudgy right hand shaded his brown eyes from the waning light of the sun sinking into the ocean's horizon.

"I think it will blow pretty soon," he groused, sucked at his teeth, and smacked his lips. "Pretty hard too, Andrew. You just wait. By Gar, if *you* don't do it, *I* will break that young fool's skull like a grape."

Olaf took off his red beret, wiped the sweat from his brow and his shaven face with his left hand, and then replaced the hat over his matted brown hair.

"Big talk, my friend," Andrew finally responded without looking up from his book. Immaculately groomed, the Frenchman sat in a collapsible, wooden deck chair in a simple, white, cotton shirt, his long legs stretched out before him in beige canvas pants and black leather boots.

The only variation in their clothing was Olaf's beret, but the difference in the two men was pronounced. The Frenchman was powerful, lean, lanky, and well manicured, with black hair receding at both temples, and a thin, trimmed mustache. He stood 6.'" tall to Olaf's 4' in height. Andrew

"Fire!"

was not only four years Olaf's senior at 36 years of age, but was a proud Frenchman through and through. His fifteen years as a mercenary had left him world-wise but not weary of life, and as tough as nails. His only two passions were himself and any woman.

Olaf, however, cared nothing about Sweden, the nation of his birth, and often lied that he was from Denmark. Olaf was a virgin and always looked unwashed. But despite their differences in life and body, Olaf and Andrew were not only close friends, but were each others only friend in a world that had orphaned both to an early life of desperate poverty, beaten them without mercy physically and emotionally, and thrown them for less than sewage in the gutter since they were both young boys.

Andrew crossed his lanky left leg over his right and cleared his throat as Olaf turned to glare at him. He sighed in resignation, lowered his book, and said: "Now be silent just for a minute, could you? I'm read...Ah. the proof of the poem. Listen to this, my stunted frend."

Andrew began to read aloud.

"When all the worlds is young, lad
And all the trees are green;
And every goose a swan, lad,
And every lass a Queen:
Then I, for boot and horse, lad,
And 'round the world away;
Young blood must have its course, lad
And every dog his day."

"That's from this book, 'The Water-Babies' by Charles Kingsley."

"At least you got the 'dog' part right," added Olaf.

Too far above them to hear Andrew's words, Dakkar released his grip from the mast, precariously balancing himself against the almost imperceptible rocking of the Nautilus. He opened his eyes and shook his head, disappointed that they could not hear him, and placed the thumb of his right hand on his cheek, cupping his remaining fingers on his chin.

"None so deaf as those who will not hear," he said for his own benefit, and began to take a series of long, deep breaths.

The dwarf ignored his captain above by looking at the blue sky of the Mediterranean.

"When I find 'Captain' Dakkar's treasure map," said Olaf contemptuously as he swaggered to the port side of the brig to stand next to three, large wooden barrels by Andrew's chair. He placed his balled fists on his hips. "I will twist the neck of that arrogant, pompous 'dog', Andrew." He blew out his cheeks and pulled his left ear with his left hand.

Reluctantly but with resignation, Legrand closed his book and reluctantly rose from his chair to join the dwarf as Olaf tiptoed to look up and over the railing of the ship.

"Arrogant?" mocked the Frenchman, twisting he tip of his left mustache with his left hand. "Arrogant? Prince Dakkar pays each of us our weight in gold for his 'folly'. But, of course, I have stumbled upon the secret of your hatred, have I not? After all, a gold *nugget*..."

"I will punch your face for one more *short joke*, Andrew!" objected the little Swede. "Your mouth betrays your ignorance...look!" he said and pointed a stubby finger at the ocean. "The ocean boils! It can't be the screw that sometimes drives the ship, it stands idle."

Raising his arms above his head, and touching fingertip to fingertip, Dakkar dove off the spar.

Leaning over the brig's gunwale next to Olaf, Andrew studied the localized turbulence in the blue-green waters directly below them and a distorted shadow beneath the surface.

"Sacre Bleu! Olaf, there are *dolphins* following the Nautilus, my friend?"

Olaf grinned at Andrew as he leaned further over the gunwale. "By gar, fate smiles at last on this simple locksmith, Andrew..."

Andrew looked at the dwarf and rolled his eyes. "*Locksmith*? Or as you say, my little man? Locksmith? You are the common pickpocket."

"*Uncommon* pickpocket to you. Alright, call me 'lock sport'. There be no dolphins in these dirty waters. But they are infested with...sharks!"

The dwarf looked up at Dakkar in mid-dive, and grinned.

"And in a minute, they will be full of shark bait named Dakkar!"

A little *pash* waterspout erupted at the point of impact of Dakkar's dive into the ocean.

"We must sound the alarm, Olaf!" the Frenchman cried out. "Dakkar faces certain death!"

"He treats me like a dirty dog," sneered Templeton. "Let the shark feast."

The dwarf turned around and took what was obviously meant to be the first of many steps away from the gunwale, but stopped suddenly to add one last insult. "They will find the 'captain' lousy fish food."

"M'sieu Olaf," groaned Andrew, "*you* are a dirty dog. You bite the hand that..."

"Oh, lucky day,' Olaf interrupted sarcastically, waving a hand in mock greeting. "My luck has taken a turn for the worse. Look, Andrew, it is Chinese bookends, Lamb and Pork Chop!"

"Hey, boys! You are just in time for the show. Dakkar is going to feed the sharks!"

Andrew glanced over his left shoulder to watch the two young men from China approaching in lock-step, identical in every detail of their being. "Their *names* are Aiguo and Bohai, except only God knows which is which."

Aiguo called out, "ut!" as Bohai added, "zut!"

As the twin brothers raised their right hands return Olaf's greeting, Legrand turned his attention back to the ocean. As the Frenchman did so, Rajesh Dakkar bobbed up on the surface of the ocean. He treaded water between the distorted shadow there and the port-side vent at the ship's stern hidden by a covering of the same wood as the hull. The unseen rotating fan in that vent spun from the force of the steam produced by the Nautilus' boiler that generated the smoke trailing from the vent.

Olaf and both China men had joined Andrew at the ship's gunwale as their captain began to swim with easy, long strokes back to the brig. Andrew's eyes widened with fear as Dakkar was suddenly jerked to a stop in mid-stroke, an expression of surprise and consternation on his face.

"Wha...?" Rajesh gasped.

He *poit* bobbed down in the water like a fisherman's cork above a hook snatched by a fish. His expression of consternation deepened into concern.

"Captain!?!" shouted the Frenchman. "Watch out!"

Dismayed, Aiguo yelled, "zukle!" as Bohai added, "mutz!"

Dakkar queried, "Andrew...?!?" and looked up at the Frenchman leaning over the side of the Nautilus just as he was *poit* yanked under the water again.

Andrew stood bolt upright and shouted, "M'sieu Henny! Get him, hurry!"

Aiguo formed a stirrup with his cupped hands and hoisted his twin to the top of the gunwale. Bohai unbuttoned his yellow, spotted vest and removed the short cleaver hidden in a leather holster against his ribs, prepared to jump overboard.

The dwarf spit over the side of the Nautilus and said, "Go ahead, jump, Pork. I bet my best lock you don't. Go ahead. Maybe I am wrong and the ship's screw *isn't* churning. Then again, maybe the sharks like sweet 'n sour pork more than Pesarattu!"

"Herr Henny!" Andrew yelled at the top of his lungs, cupping both hands at the corners of his mouth. "Henny! On deck...with your harpoon! The Prince...!"

The Frenchman felt a tug on the left leg of his canvas pants and glanced down into the disappointed face of the dwarf.

"No, Andrew, no," Olaf said, without inflection as small circles rippled out at the point where Dakkar had been jerked beneath the ocean. "Don't make noise, you drunken frog! Herr Henny might harpoon the shark!"

"M'sieu Olaf! How can a man even such as you live with blood on his hand?!" asked Andrew. "Have you *no* shame?"

"I will live in the palace on the king's preserves in Stockholm, filthy rich, when I find Dakkar's map. As for blood...By Gar, Andrew, blood *will* stain this deck..."

It was then that Dakkar and Indra Singh popped like corks out of the water "*Bwhahaha!*" laughing and sputtering.

"The only question is whose...Damn!" Olaf contemptuously added as he saw Singh and Rajesh Dakkar bobbing in the ocean. "Damn and double-damn! It's Dakkar's bald-headed flunky, Singh Song, *and* the idiot captain! Why do bad things always happen to this good little pick-pocket?"

Laughing, Aiguo snatched up a thick, rope ladder of hemp coiled by the barrels and tied one end to one of the many recessed rings in the deck. He threw the rest of the rope overboard.

"Odqnrk!' he said and began to lower it over the side of the ship as Bohai returned his cleaver to the inside of his vest, buttoned it, and hopped down from the gunwale.

In the same moment, Olaf unbuttoned the lower third of his shirt, revealing a leather strap that circled his belly. Dozens of loops on the strap held his lock picking tools. Grumbling, his removed the lock and its key that he'd earlier placed in the left, front pocket of his jeans, and attached the skeleton key to the strap. He re-buttoned his shirt.

He kissed it and then threw the lock over the side of the ship.

Grumbling, the dwarf climbed with some effort to the top of a barrel. As he did so, he noticed two, thick, folded towels on the second and two sets of clothing on the third barrel and realized they belonged to Dakkar and Singh. The idea to toss them overboard brought a smile to his face.

Bohai helped Dakkar as Andrew helped Singh climb over the railing and onto the deck.

"Chop!" Rajesh Dakkar said and chuckled.

"M'sieu Legrand? Are we children needing help?"

"*Sacre Bleu*, we thought that you were as good as dead!" Andrew answered and winked.

"Some of us," sneered Olaf, standing atop his barrel, his hands defiantly on his hips, "think of you dead as good." He leaned over, picked up the towels, and tossed them to Aiguo. "Did you know about this stupid prank, Andrew?"

"Oui. Of course, Mr. Templeton, you pin-headed dunderhead. I guess the joke is on you!"

"Har, har. I thought you were my friend." Olaf jumped off the barrel. "I was wrong."

"Hulck," added Aiguo, and handed a towel to Dakkar. "Pdmswbd."

"Is this Mr. Templeton 'the jolly.'" asked Rajesh Dakkar as he accepted the towel and began to vigorously dry his matted hair. "Still angry over 'meager' pay, sorry food, the direction of the wind, how your hair lay on the side of your head when you got out of bed this morning...or has your list of grievances swollen?"

"He is happy only when he is unhappy, my Prince," observed Singh as he spread his towel on the deck by Andrew's chair. "It is his nature to be *short* tempered."

Rajesh chuckled, stepped out of his loincloth, and dropped it to the deck. He said, "I was *short*-sighted, wasn't I, Singh Song. I forgot to mention his demanding Herr Henny's expulsion."

"Women..." said Olaf referring to Henny as he took out a toothpick from the right pocket of his pants that found its usual home between his lips, "...are bad luck on a boat."

"Ignorant drivel, Mr. Templeton. Give me one reason Henderickson Lagle shouldn't be here," Rajesh said as he stretched out on his stomach on his towel next to Indra Singh.

Olaf removed his tooth pick and turned his head to find the source of the voice behind him. Both Dakkar and Singh rose up on their forearms where they lay and followed Olaf's gaze.

"I think 'he' can speak for 'herself', eh Herr Henny?"

Initially standing several yards away from his fellows, Henderickson "Henny" Lagle began to approach Olaf, Rajesh, Singh, and the Chops with a swagger that only added to the impression of a big, proud man of Prussian nobility and impeccable grooming. He seemed perfectly at ease and unaffected in a long-sleeved, blue velvet robe with Egyptian symbols on its lapel and on bands at its wrists. His mane of blond hair, his blond walrus mustache, and bushy blond eyebrows only accented his masculinity.

"Did someone request the harpoon?" added the Prussian, patting the barrel of the musket in the crook of his right arm. "This 'harpoon' is a Pottsdam musket, just converted to a percussion piece. She ist 56 1/2" of deadly accuracy, and last served a soldier in the Napoleonic Wars. That soldier could put a shot through the eye of a shark at one hundred paces and make the shark like it."

Henny placed the palm of his right hand on his right cheek, and pretending to blush.

"Oh, there I go again, talking of me *again*. Well, so be it."

Rajesh rose from his towel, picked it up, and, standing naked before Henny, began to vigorously dry his hair with it.

"Herr Henny! Pleasant surprise!" he said, smiling. "I hope you don't expect false modesty."

"*Sahib*...." Indra whispered sharply as he rose from his own towel and began wrapping it around his hips. "Please. Don't."

"Ach du lieber!" quipped Henny as he looked with satiric derision at Rajesh. "Such 'perfection' *demands* praise, gentlemen..."

Henny looked at his open right hand as if he were studying the whorls on his fingertips. He said, "But I ban not disappointed, 'mighty Prince'. I *expected* false pride."

The smile died on Rajesh's face as Singh laughed into the palm of his own hand.

"But modesty" Henny continued, shaking his head like a lion tossing its mane, "stills my tongue. Oh dear, was I talking about *me*, again?

"I think it will blow pretty soon, pretty hard, boys!" Olaf said and began to chortle as Rajesh, hiding his perturbation behind a blank expression, yanked his shirt off the barrel where it lay.

"Sahib," scolded Singh as he pulled on his canvas pants, "is there no boundary you will not test, no code you hold sacred? No man should be embarrassed by his captain in front of others."

"Please, Singh Song," said Dakkar as he continued dressing. "No lecture today. I didn't exactly kill someone, you know. It was only an innocent joke."

"The lust of the eyes in no trivial matter, no matter what its object, my Lord. It is a sin. And please don't call me that."

"I am not 'your Lord', Indra, as I've told you a million times. Please.... call me Dakkar, or Rajesh Dakkar, but not your lord or master. And as for sin, that's a God thing, and you are well aware that I, your student and friend, am a godless heathen."

"Donnervetter, Singh has no sense of humor," observed Henny. "Neither does the captain. Then again, neither do I."

"And the wages of sin," continued Indra, ignoring both Dakkar's indifference and Henny's ironic statement, "is death." He pressed the palms of his hands together at his chest in an attitude of fervent prayer.

"Ach du lieber! *Another* sermon? Time for this magnificent mercenary to go to bed." And so saying, solemn and resigned that his relationship with Singh would never change, the Prussian mercenary sauntered away, saying, "And worse than that, going alone."

Singh swabbed his bald pate from front to back with his right hand, then shook his head in disbelief. From long habit, he finished dressing in his Kunta; a collarless, beige, long-sleeved tunic that fell to mid-calf over his pants. Then, bending at his waist, he first pulled on his left and then his right black boot. He looked up at Rajesh and decided to speak his mind against his better judgment.

"I am still dumbfounded," he said, "by your choice of men for your expedition, sahib. They are a circus of misfits; a dwarf who's main talent is jumping from prison to prison, two mute China men whose tongues were cut out by their Emperor, a French cad whose only fame is escaping from the bedrooms of the husbands he's cuckolded, and a Prussian mercenary and sharp-shooter who was between wars, I mean, jobs. Could you really find no better candidates for your "Black Knights.'"

"Aye," responded Rajesh as he finished buttoning his shirt. "But this 'circus' will pick, vault over, or even shoot off any 'lock' or overcome any obstacle that might stop me from fulfilling my goal."

He shook his head, disappointed. "Singh, Singh. There is none so blind as he who will not see."

As he often did, Rajesh placed the thumb of his right hand on his cheek and cupped his remaining fingers on his chin. As he did so and unseen by anyone, a door to the ship's pantry below deck slowly runked open just a crack on an inky, wire-haired, squatting, ravenous thing of yellow, slobbering fangs and green eyes burning with a hellish fire.

Chapter Seven

The opened door to the pantry runked closed.

"Sirs," announced Captain Dakkar to his expeditionary crew that was scattered in clusters across the deck, "return to your rooms or your stations, as is appropriate. The show is over for today."

Rajesh turned to face his mentor. "Singh, remind yourself to call them to deck first light in their new uniforms. It's time to start turning this ragtag bunch of misfits into a topnotch team. We will start with exercises, and then proceed to a demonstration by each man of his particular talent."

"Sahib," asked Indra, "may I speak freely?"

"As do all free men," sighed Dakkar as he watched Andrew and Olaf walk away down the starboard side of the Nautilus and the two Chop's marching in step away from him on the port side.

Singh continued, "I must say it again. You should not have ridiculed Herr Henny, sahib."

"Ridiculed?!" Rajesh objected as he began to move to the port gunwale of his brig. "Singh?! I have no prejudice against his kind. After eighteen years together, I'd think you'd know that."

"You also talk down to your men, Rajesh. I know that you don't consider yourself better than any other man. But you do it nevertheless, and you lose their respect, and how can any leader demand obedience without respect?"

Dakkar leaned forward, his forearms on the gunwale of the ship, and looked out over the calm sea at the sinking sun. Singh imitated his stance.

"You are overly sensitive, Singh. Always have been. I speak at their level, my friend. Your imagination runs wild. I believe it is going to be a beautiful night. Just enjoy it."

"Ah, how I love the smell of the ocean, the salt on the breeze, and that strange, yellow light as the sun sets that makes everything seem fey. Don't you? It's almost enough to get me to believe in mermaids, sea serpents, and sunken cities full of gold and fabulous jewels."

"Your ship is rife with rumors, sahib Dakkar," Singh contained, ignoring his captain's revere. "They fear the unknown, as do all men. *Some* of them *do* believe in mermaids and sea serpents."

"More superstitious nonsense. Then let them seek enlightenment, Singh."

Below deck, a cook's assistant opened the door to the ship's pantry. He wore the cloth hat and single-breasted, long-sleeved shirt buttoned down its right side worn by the crew of the Nautilus. Pausing in its threshold, he took out a match from his right pant pocket and struck it on the doorjamb. He stepped inside, holding the match high.

He began to whistle as he removed the glass globe from the whale-oil lamp bolted to the wall next to the doorway, lit its wick, and replaced the globe. He fanned the flame of the match out and let it fall to the floor. The lamp gave rise to as much flickering shadow as light as he entered the well-stocked pantry full of secured, wooden crates and containers, sometimes stacked higher than his head.

Above deck, Indra Singh continued to advise Rajesh whose patience was wearing thin.

"You keep our purpose and destination a secret," continued Indra. "Like a man walking alone through a graveyard in the dead of night, they say anything *not* to hear *their* voices...but to cover voices *they cannot hear.*"

"Superstitious nonsense. What they know must suffice, Singh. I'll not jeopardize this mission over imaginary monsters. And all will be revealed to them soon enough."

Below deck, the cook found the crate of foodstuffs he'd wanted. He reached up to remove it from its shelf when *shusks* the silence of the storage room was broken. His hand froze in mid-reach.

"It's probably a rat," he whispered to himself.

The cook slowly looked over his right shoulder, his eyes dilated with fear.

Instantly, a clawed, wire-haired *hand* from some horror behind him clutched his throat, choking him, tearing at his flesh.

The cook gurgled *ukk* once as he struggled against the vicious attack. His hand fell from the crate as a second clawed horror joined the first on his neck.

The cook fought with every ounce of his being to tear the hands from his throat as tiny dots of blood formed where each claw sank into his neck. Wide eyed with confusion and fear, he threw out his useless hands, clutching for only God knew what as red spots swam before his eyes. He knocked one of the crates off of the shelving.

The clawed hand jerked his head *back* against another box, knocking off the cook's cloth cap.

The cook's struggle began to weaken as his windpipe was crushed.

The clawed hand jerked his head back against the crate, breaking its staves and throwing two other containers to the floor.

With his last fragment of a breath, the cook cried out, "Yakutsk!"

Above deck, Rajesh jerked upright from the railing. "Wha...! Singh!? Did you hear that?!"

With terrific force, the horror behind him *slammed* the cook's head back against the crate a third time, shattering the cook's head and rocking the shelf.

"It comes from the hold!" said Singh as he and Rajesh started to run across the deck.

"Templeton! Henny! Andrew!" yelled Dakkar at the top of his lungs as they ran. "*All* hands to the hold! All hands to the hold! Now!"

In less than a minute, Indra and Rajesh stood clustered in the threshold of the open door to the pantry. Henny already knelt over the body of the cook. It was limp as a bloody rag doll, laying among a chaos of broken and fallen crates of food. Even in the flickering light cast by the single lamp that the cook had lit, the two men saw blood sloughing from the cook's broken nose and two bloody gashes in his pallid right cheek.

"What happened, Herr Henny?" asked Dakkar. "Is he alive?"

"There is *blood*, sahib," gasped Indra Singh behind him. He swabbed his bald pate from front to back with his right hand as they both stepped cautiously into the pantry.

"It is the cook...." whispered Lagle, glancing rapidly around the cluttered pantry. "The cook."

Now the dwarf stood on the threshold of the doorway, rubbing his right eye with his right hand. "By gar, what is all the ruckus? Just when I was good asleep."

"Hogwash, Mr. Templeton" said Rajesh. "You didn't have enough time to take off your socks. We heard a noise."

"There has been an accident, Templeton," added Singh as Olaf approached Henny and the body of the cook. "We just arrived."

"I was in quarters," said Henny, rising from the cook's body, "and heard a scream loud enough to wake the dead. I was the first one here, and saw no one leaving."

Olaf knelt by the cook and held two of the fingers of his right hand on the cook's neck.

"Not loud enough to wake this one, Henny," he said and looked up. "Nothing will be waking up this one. He has been '*accidentally*' murdered."

Rajesh joined Olaf on the floor by the body and, gently cradling the cook's head in his right hand, carefully studied the dead man's wounds. Finished with his diagnosis, he laid the cook's head carefully back on the floor. "I swear by all that his holy; the man who did this will pay dearly."

Singh arched his left eyebrow. "*You* think something is *holy*. And what might that be?"

"He's right, Herr Henny. This was no accident," added Rajesh, ignoring Singh as he waved his right arm at the jumbled crates on the floor. "My first guess is that one of those boxes may have been used as the weapon. That his head was bludgeoned against a crate."

Rajesh rose and moved to the shattered crate closest to the cook's body. As he analyzed its broken staves, Olaf stomped over to Henny, placed his hands on his hips, and scowled.

"There is blood and hair on the edge of this one," continued Dakkar.

"Something behind this crate with ragged fingernails or claws grabbed the cook by his neck, there are small, bloody cuts there, and jerked his head back against it to crush his skull."

Olaf looked up at Henny and shook a pudgy finger at the Prussian.

"What?" he sneered, pulling his ear with his left hand. "No accidental murder, Dakkar? Then maybe he was killed by 'superstitious nonsense' or an 'imaginary monster' from *Germany*, by gar."

"Himmel!" the Prussian exploded, his face flushed red and his hands balled into fists. "You are too great a coward to directly call me a murderer, you shrunken monkey!?!"

Henny snatched Olaf off of the floor.

"Put me down!" yelled Olaf, squirming in Henny's powerful grip. "Put me down, you overgrown pig, or I'll...!"

"You want down, you squirmin' little monkey?! *I'll...*" growled the Prussian, and released his grip, "...put you down!"

Olaf fell *thud* to the floor, and howled, "Dammit! That hurt!"

The dwarf jumped up and furiously waved his right fist at the Prussian as he stomped towards the pantry door. But before he could reach it, Singh grabbed his left arm and restrained the furious dwarf.

"I think it will blow pretty soon," the dwarf yelled, "and pretty hard for *you*, you German slut!"

"Mr. Templeton," warned Singh, "stop this. You're acting like a child."

"I am *Prussian*, you blithering idiot," Henny muttered as he stomped to and then past Singh and Olaf, and then through the door. "You had best remember that!"

"Herr Henny!" Singh called after him as he released Olaf and took a first step to follow the Prussian. "Herr Henny, come back!" But Rajesh placed the palm of his right hand on his chest to stop him from following after the marksman.

"Let him go, Indra Singh. There is no blood on his hands or clothing. It is impossible that he killed this sailor. But your words will not wash the pain from his heart."

Singh hesitated.

"I will instruct the crew," continued Rajesh, "to prepare the body for burial. Tell the men to arm themselves. Until we find the assassin, everyone uses caution tonight."

Rajesh leaned close to Singh and whispered in his ear. "It's time to take Mr. Templeton aside for *the talk*, my friend. I will see you in my stateroom after."

Rajesh winked and walked to the door with Olaf following close behind.

"Put me down, you overgrown pig…"

But before the dwarf reached the exit, Singh seized his right shoulder.

Olaf barked, "What the hell..." and jerked his shoulder free." No one puts a hand on me! I am Olaf Templeton!"

"*I* am the Hell," Singh said, and, grabbing the back of his shirt and pants, jerked Templeton back into the room. "You aren't going anywhere." Dead sober, Singh knelt by the struggling dwarf, face to face, and raised his right hand with his index finger and thumb barely parted.

"Mr. Templeton, you are about *this close* to being tossed overboard by everybody on the Nautilus *except* by the man you seem to hate the most. *Henny's* vote was no. So you are left with a choice to make. You stay and talk to me, or you catch a ride on the next shark back to the coast."

"No one talks that way to me," Olaf contemptuously snarled. "I performed for the kings and queens of Europe. I was the headliner in the Piccadilly Circus in London."

"You were a performer in a flea-bitten carnival, Mr. Templeton" said Indra, "who made more money from picking pockets than from performing on stage, and who spent more time in jail than he spent dressed as 'The Hottentot Pygmy' in the carnival's freak show."

"That's a bold-faced lie!" Olaf snarled. "I was no Hottentot anything! I am a locksport!"

Ignoring Olaf's invective, Singh continued, "Over my objections, Prince Dakkar sent me to hire you for your well-known 'skills' with a lock, not for your moral integrity, and I found you and bailed you out of jail in Budapest for stealing a large amount of money from a safe that was found on your person. Prince Dakkar is paying you a King's Ransom to become a team member of this expedition, with a promise of a huge bonus if we succeed. Choose now. Do you stay and listen to what I have to say, or go?"

Olaf looked down at the floor, his chin on his chest, and shuffled his feet for a long moment before reluctantly looking up into Indra eyes. "Dakkar talk down to me. He thinks he is superior."

Singh released him and closed the door to the pantry.

"Prince Dakkar *is* superior to you and everyone on this ship, including me, and possibly to everyone on earth at this moment in history. What he doesn't invent, he improves, like the American Robert Fulton's steam engine. He took Fulton's smokestack and turned it into the huge vents on the port and starboard sides of our stern, and turned Fulton's steam-driven wheel into a screw at the stern and bottom of the Nautilus that drives us forward at incredible speed when it is in use. In fact, there are dozens of such unique or greatly modified devices aboard the Nautilus that exist no where else on Earth, Olaf. What did *you* invent lately? A new skeleton key? A new way to lift a penny from the purse of Queen Lydia, the bearded lady?"

"Rajesh is a genius. Therefore, it is *natural* for him to act like a genius, just as a fish swims like a fish and an eagle flies without thinking about flying. What you think is arrogance is just his nature, the nature of genius. And despite what you think, he doesn't act out of pride or a sense of superiority. In fact, he believes firmly in the equality of all men. Given that, do you stay and listen, or go?"

Olaf took off his beret and slapped it against his thigh. As he replaced it on his head, he said, "It's not like I have a real choice. Say your piece."

Singh looked at the uncanny corpse of the cook and said, "Not here, Olaf. We should respect the dead. I'll walk you to your cabin."

Olaf grudgingly nodded in agreement, Singh reopened the door, and both men left the pantry.

"My piece is this," Singh continued as they walked up the stairs that lead to the deck above. "Dakkar hired you as a member of his expeditionary *team* to do a job. He doesn't carry about your past. He doesn't care about your religion, or your politics, or your opinions. What he wants is no more snide remarks, no more hate-filled looks, no more resistance to everything he asks of you. He wants the same for every other member of the 'Black Knights' as well. Do your job, join the team. Get rid of the bad attitude. Put that in your back pocket until we are done, then you can go back to being Olaf the Nasty on your own time. Do you understand what I'm saying?"

"I'm not stupid. I understand. And if I don't, what will really happen?"

"No bonus, and you'll be chained in the hold until we return to India."

For long, pensive moments, their footfalls were the only sound on the deck. Then the dwarf broke the silence. "It's not like I have a choice. I'll do it."

Singh sighed. "Good. There's only one more thing."

Olaf looked up, indignant. "Ha! Ha! I *knew* there had to be more. What 'one thing.'"

Singh looked down at the dwarf and smiled. "Two things, actually. Stop saying 'I think it will blow pretty soon, pretty hard'. And don't call me 'Singh Song' again. It's really irritating."

A gibbous white moon hung, smug, against the hushed, black of the night sky above the Nautilus, its sails still tightly furled. As it gently rocked, reflected stars danced and cavorted around and below the brig.

No cloud marred the horizon, and, except the creaking of the ship, silence hung like a shroud over the brig.

Like hand slaps, two muted retorts rang out across the waves, violating the silence. There was a pregnant pause, and then another set of *Bang Bang*!

Henny Lagle, dressed in an American buckskin shirt fringed across its chest and at its seams at its shoulders, stood behind the helmsman of the Nautilus. He aimed the pistol in his right hand at an imaginary foe, someone on the deck of the ship, and, for the third time, said, "*Bang! Bang!*"

"'Don't waste bullets', he says," Henny groused. "The captain thinks I'm a child. I was shooting the eyes out of gnats when he was in diapers!"

"They think the cook found Dakkar's treasure map," said the helmsman whose rough hands were firm and sure on the ship's helm. His eyes were on the black ocean before him, not on the Prussian, as he spoke. "The ship's crew, that is. And that *you* killed him for that map, Herr Henny."

Beneath his greatcoat and a traditional sailor's beige cap with a blue anchor stitched under its upturned lip, the helmsman wore the uniform of the ship's crew; a uniform designed by Rajesh.

"Then the crew are idiots." Henny aimed the pistol. "Who needs the map? He takes us *to* the treasure. I think Mr. Templeton killed him over 'short rations'. Hehe. Hehehe. Short rations; get it?"

"*Bang.*"

The helmsman laughed quietly. "You're a funny fellow for a German mercenary. Just how many men *have* you killed?"

"Not enough." Henny holstered his pistol in the belt slung over his left shoulder. "I am the funny fellow for the *Prussian*, and my shift is over. You have been protected. And I am an old and exhausted marksman and headed for bed. See you in the morning."

"Aye, in the morning," repeated the helmsman without turning. "Hahaha. Can't say I blame Olaf. I could use a handful of Solomon's diamonds myself. Good night and good rest, my friend."

Behind him, the claw almost imperceptibly clicked on the damp, wooden deck.

"Good night and good riddance," answered Henny as he disappeared into the dark.

Uncertain that he heard anything, the helmsman said, "Eh...?!" and turned his head over his left shoulder to find the source of the faint sound. Failing to do so and writing it off to imagination, he said, "Henny?" Is that..."

It snarled, vicious.

"Henny?" Is that..." the helmsman began again, his voice uneasy.

In that second, all yellow, burning eyes and slobbering fangs, framed by the moon behind and above, the ravenous werewolf screamed and leapt

"...you," the helmsman whispered as his cap fell off and he threw his arms up against the hellish face of death.

Chapter Eight

"Did Mr. Templeton accept or reject our little ultimatum, Singh?" asked Rajesh as he squatted by his roll-top, mahogany desk; a treasured gift from his father for his eighteenth birthday. He had pulled it slightly away from the wall of his stateroom. Above the meticulously organized desk and bolted to the wall, a whale-oil lamp threw odd, wavering shadows and too little light over the room. Its fishy stink was subtle. In the wall behind the desk was the opened door of a safe.

"He said he would do it, but I don't believe him," said Indra Singh in silhouette and standing in the doorway, looking back down the corridor leading to Dakkar's stateroom. "I don't trust anything that little miscreant says. His oaths are worthless."

"Oh?" said Dakkar as he closed the safe and stood up. He held a long, cardboard tube in his hands. "And just *why* don't you trust him?"

"He stole my wallet."

Rajesh chuckled and moved to his daybed by his desk.

"Well, it isn't all bad news, Singh. At least you weren't beaten to death by the monster on board. How could any human being murder another? I swear, my old friend, that, despite my best efforts, I don't really understand the black hearts of some people."

"There *is* consolation in still being alive and in another beautiful night..." said Singh, turning to face his student, friend, and captain, "fashioned by God's merciful hand."

"Don't let me squelch your thirst after metaphysical nonsense, Singh," said Dakkar as he sat on his bed and opened an end of the tube, "but what consoles our *dead cook* about tonight, eh? Was he blessed tonight by that same invisible God?"

"I forgive your denial of the Living God as the folly of youth," said Indra, approaching his captain. "That folly is to mistake reading a book about horses with riding a horse, my Lord. We each must *experience* God to fully understand. And I would remind you to think before you speak. The beginning of wisdom is the fear of God."

"Again, and hopefully for the final time, don't call me your 'Lord' or 'Prince', 'Singh Song'. My name, as you well know, is Rajesh Dakkar. And the beginning of wisdom is the search for knowledge, not imaginary gods."

Inside the tube were several tightly coiled maps. Rajesh carefully removed and unrolled one of them then tossed the tube to the far side of his bed.

"The knowledge I seek lies hidden in this map, Singh. It is the first step on what promises to be a long but rewarding adventure. But I'll concede I doubted my own quest not so long ago..."

Dakkar spread the map on the daybed, and pointed his left index finger at Delhi, India. He placed the thumb of his right hand on his cheek and cupped his remaining fingers on his chin

"...in Delhi. After all, of what use is knowledge to a dead man? And I came pretty close to being that corpse."

The old beggar sat like a corpse in a ragged turban and tattered robe on the steps leading up to an ancient, three-storied building behind him that looked like its open galleries, columns, balconies, arched windows, abutments and twin domes had been chiseled out of the side of a rock quarry. A main thoroughfare of the city ended at the foot of the stairs where the old man sat, and two rows of much smaller buildings housing various businesses lined both sides of the dusty boulevard. Looking like gnats riding the heat waves rising from the ground, a handful of shop owners and customers milled around the street and in front of the businesses. That handful was peppered by ragamuffin children busy at exploring life.

As the beggar looked down that thoroughfare, his left hand held a rough cudgel between his legs that rested on a step. Lines of sweat that began just below his stained, dirty turban above his wrinkled forehead trickled down into a ragged, grey beard. He did not smell clean.

The beggar turned his head at the sound of footfalls above him to watch a hooded and robed figure descending the crumbling stone stairs behind him. His impatience was obvious.

"Sahib?" asked the inscrutable person of indeterminate sex who stopped on the step above him.

"You have the map?" the beggar asked. "I have waited too long, and the day is blistering hot."

"How deep is your thirst, old man?" a voice from the depths of the hood asked as its left hand removed a cardboard tube from the folds of its robe. The old man rose with some effort from his step to accept the offered container.

Suddenly, the beggar saw two turbaned men appear behind the map's owner. One of the men named Samta seized his right arm.

"Get the map!" Samta snarled at his cohort, Aiemapt, who was threatening the beggar with a long, deadly knife by brandishing it in the air. "Hurry!"

"*You* make *one* stinking sound," Samta spat at the unfortunate object of his threat, "or make one wrong move, and you're as good as dead, you lousy traitor."

"How deep *is* your thirst, old man?" Aiemapt hissed at the beggar, still waving his blade. "Is it as deep as this knife?"

"Too much talk," said a *third* turbaned man who, appearing behind Aiemapt and leaning forward, *snatched* the tube away from the beggar.

"Hey!" the beggar yelled, grabbing at but failing to seize his attacker's arm. "What the hell are you doing! That's mine!"

He swung his cudgel at the thug, but missed, and lost his grip. The cudgel spun away to clatter down the steps.

"Long live Nechops...!" growled the third thug, Serapis, clutching the map, and shoved the 'traitor' away who huffed and stumbled against Samta.

Aiemapt punched the face hidden by its hood. "Long live the Most Exalted High Custodian of the Library of Alexandria!" His victim fell, sitting, to the steps.

"Shut up!" screamed Serapis. "Let's get out of here!"

Instantly, the three assailants, Serapis still clutching the stolen tube as Aiemapt sheathed his knife in his belt, broke away from their victim and began to jump down the steps.

"Why the hell did you say your name, you fool?!" snarled Serapis as they descended.

There was no answer as the outraged old beggar tottered after them, shaking his fists.

Their flight down the steps into the street was as quick as it was certain.

"Stop them!" the beggar yelled to the people around him. "Stop them!" But the milling crowd in the street either did not hear or pretended deafness. The thieves were already well ahead of the old beggar as they dodged between or around the maze of people in the narrow street. As they ran, Samta bumped hard into the shoulder of a bystander, throwing him off balance.

"Hey, what's this?!?" he shouted as two merchant's watched indifferently from the doorway of a shop. As the thieves ran, their hooded target staggered up and, with faltering steps, began to pursue the thieves who were only several yards behind the beggar.

"They're following us, Serapis!" gasped Aiempt to his cohort with the map. He glanced over his shoulder at his two victims running close behind and gaining on them. Merchants and customers alike that had finally realized what was happening in the past few seconds now tried to escape the mayhem in the street by ducking into alleys and doorways. Mothers grabbed up children.

The thieves staggered into a flock of pigeons grazing for crumbs of refuse that exploded up in a cloud of wings and beaks as they passed.

"Get out of the way!" yelled Serapis at the birds as he simultaneously and viciously shoved a surprised shopper out of his way who barked, "Son of a…!".

As he ran, Serapis passed the tube to Samta.

Abruptly, the three thieves turned sharply into another alley. Above them, a woman leaned out of the second story window of her home and sloushed the day's bucket of garbage into the street below, drenching Serapis and breaking his stride.

Startled, he looked up in mid-step, sputtered and yelled, "Hey! What the...!?!" Left behind by his two fellow thugs and wiping garbage from his eyes, Serapis staggered hard into a red brick wall, moaned, and then collapsed, unconscious, to the street.

Ignorant of Serapis' fate and spying an open doorway ahead of them in the alley, Aiempt turned to Samta and huffed, "We've...lost... them...in here, *quick*."

Samta turned his head to respond. "By Allah's beard, I thought we…" and collided against the barrel chest of a huge man whose booted feet were firmly planted on the street. A fraction of a second later, Aiempt rammed into Samta.

Flattened against his body, Samta looked up into the sober face of Indra Singh.

Aiempt muttered, "Allah! What..?"

Singh seized both thugs by the backs of their necks and raised them almost without effort in his massive hands, kicking and gasping, off of their sandaled feet.

"The wages of sin," he said, "is death." and Aiempt and Samta believed him.

"Hyuck…uck." Samta gurgled, gasping for breath and still clutching the tube as he dangled from Singh's right hand. His turban fell from his head to the street.

"Uk..uk..uk." Aiempat gurgled, his knife, his vanity, his strength, and his courage forgotten as he hung from Singh's left hand. His eyes began to bulge.

"Consider this a *partial* payment," Singh added with the voice of finality. "The full amount delayed from my undeserved mercy."

Effortlessly, Singh cracked *thud* their heads together, then let Samta and Aiempat drop, limp and unconscious, at his feet as the beggar and the hooded owner of the tube approached him.

"For a… moment…I…thought all was…lost." said the old man. "Good job, Singh!"

"Just who is this?" asked the mysterious hooded figure looking up at Singh who was clapping the palms of his great hands as if he were cleaning chalk from erasers.

"I am Indra," Singh answered, extending a hand in friendship. "Indra Singh. The third thief lies unconscious in a pool of sewage at the mouth of the alley.

"How can I ever thank you?" asked the hooded enigma.

"You cannot," answered Rajesh's mentor. "We should leave before they awaken." Then he pressed the palms of his hands together at his chest in an attitude of prayer. "We should leave now."

"Singh!" said the beggar, kneeling to retrieve the tube, "Singh! This is it!"

He opened one end of the tube and partially withdrew a rolled-up scroll. On the side of the tube was written…

"Inside," said the beggar,"is power beyond imagination!"

Excited and with his eyes glued to the map, the old man rose from his right knee to his full height. "I will hold a fire that does not burn!"

"The one at the mouth of the alley," said Singh, pointing with his right arm, "the thief covered with garbage is running away, my Lord."

"No matter," said the old man, studying the writing on the tube. "Let him go. Let them all go. They have served their purpose."

"You word is my act, Rajesh," said Singh.

"The price for that 'fire' was steep, old man," said the thug's intended victim. The hood was pushed back from a beautiful, brown face with large, blue, almond-shaped eyes, a comely nose, and full lips beneath a wealth of thick, black hair that fell to her neck. The back of her right hand lying at the base of her neck was painted with an open eye and the Egyptian symbol for eternity, the Ankh, centered in its pupil.

Tears welled in her eyes as she said, "The cost was betrayal."

Dakkar looked up at Singh from the map where it lay on his daybed.

"Now *her* life, not yours, is in danger, sahib," said Indra Singh. "What will you do with it?"

"She is in a safe place that I cannot even share with you, old friend. She is like Prometheus," Rajesh continued. "Her betrayal brings fire to man."

"Or Sahib Dakkar to destruction," said Singh, shaking his head from shoulder to shoulder in disappointment. "Your youth, master, continues to lead you into dangerous territory, at best."

"Ah. You suspect a staged theft in Delhi, sir?" Dakkar smiled. "Your cynicism surprises me. Impossible. I was disguised. As an old beggar. Remember?"

"You have been buying rare books," said Singh, "from across the world for over ten years. Your...*interest*...and name are not unknown."

"My name maybe well known, but my face remains a mystery to all but a few, so my statement must stand. Even the thug who escaped only knows a giant bald man foiled his attempted theft."

"All but the *woman* who *sold you* the map, Rajesh. She certainly saw your face, and knows your name. If she betrayed her own people, which she did, why would she not betray *you* as..."

A knock at Dakkar's door interrupted Singh's thought. He took the few steps needed to reach the door as Rajesh rolled up the map and picked up its tube.

"The Soters are a cloistered, secret order," said Rajesh as he began to replace the rolled map back in its tube. "I doubt they know Bundlekund exists outside some outdated text. Answer the door, old teacher. Your point is well taken.

"But," Dakkar added as Indra took the latch of the door in hand, "*if* the shortest route to a destination is to swallow the bait, the wise fish bites the hook."

The knock at the door sounded again.

"Wait," said the prince as he recapped the tube. He walked back to his desk and knelt by the safe, deposited the tube then closed the door of the safe, locked it, and rose. He quietly pushed his desk back against the wall.

"You may open it now, Singh."

"Who disturbs the captain," Indra Singh asked, opening the door a crack, "at this late hour?"

"Mr. Templeton's scapegoat, Henny Lagle."

Singh opened the door on Henny, still in his buckskin shirt, his head hung in shame.

"I come to save the dwarf the effort," said the marksman. "I killed your helmsman, Captain Dakkar."

The full moon hung yet higher in the star splatter sky as Aiguo and Bohai, Olaf, Andrew, and several other crew members of the Nautilus clustered around the mangled corpse of the helmsman as Dakkar, Henny, and Singh approached them.

"Oh, God, I feel sick," said one of the ship's crew as he clutched his stomach with his left hand and partially covered his mouth with the spread fingers of his right hand. "Oh, oh, oh, my gut."

Rajesh pushed him and a second crew member lightly aside to reach the body. As he did so, he barked, "Stand aside, sirs! I need room to examine the body."

The sailor ran to the closest gunwale, doubled over at the waist, and vomited over the side.

"Yumpin' Yimney!" Olaf uttered, his right hand partially covering his own mouth as he stood next to Andrew. Puzzled and afraid, the dwarf stared at the dead sailor. "His throat! His head!"

"Sacre Bleu," whispered Andrew. "The blood is..."

Aiguo and Bohai lowered their grief stricken faces in respect for the dead as Dakkar knelt by the corpse, laying his right hand gingerly on the dead man's stomach. Three slashes had shredded the helmsman's clothing there.

"ulk," they both said in unison. "gractyh."

A small pool of fresh but tacky blood had spread under the helmsman's broken head.

"He was murdered by 'accidental superstition' too, yah?" sneered Olaf with his pudgy fists now firmly planted on his hips. "Yah? *I* say he was murdered by the *captain's* negligence..."

"Mr. Templeton!' Singh warned the dwarf with fire in his eyes. "Our agreement...!"

"I *could be* wrong, I guess," Olaf added, pulling his ear with his left hand.

"He was slaughtered by a werewolf," said Henny slapping his right thigh for emphasis, "Or I am a monkey's uncle. Just look at the slashes on his neck."

"That's enough, gentlemen" stated Dakkar, decisively. He rose from the body. "You are acting like frightened children. "

"The slashes are clean and uniform, not ragged. An animal's claws mangle. In addition, his head was repeatedly bashed against the deck after he fell. He was not killed by a wolf. He was not killed by an imaginary werewolf. He was killed by a man."

"By Gar, this is *your proof*, 'Captain.'" asked Olaf, the expression on his face again awash with anger and disbelief. "The other crew member, the cook, had the same slashes! This is the work of a monster with superhuman strength. This is the work of a werewolf."

"Then further proof would be tonight's full moon, eh, Mr. Templeton?" said Dakkar and turned to face the dwarf. "Herr Lagle? *Everyone* knows a man becomes a wolf under its light, right?"

"Ja...ja" said Henny cautiously, then the corners of his mouth below his heavy walrus mustache slowly drew us into a smile. "Ja! That is right!"

"Then where are *Herr Henny's* claws, Mr. Templeton? So that at least eliminates Henny, your *first* suspect, eh?   M'sieu Andrew! Please call *everyone* on deck. Now."

"Oui, Cap'n," said the Frenchman, and he gingerly stepped around the helmsman's dead body to walk to the helm and the voice tube bracketed to it. Its flexible, rubber hose ran down to and disappeared below the deck through a hole. Andrew removed the cone of the tube, placed his mouth close to it, and cupped his hand around his mouth.

"All hands on zee deck! All hands on zee deck!" he bellowed. "Double quick!"

As he did so, Rajesh turned to two of the ship's crew already present and said, "Michael, Robert, go quickly below deck and get a cloth to cover our poor murdered brother. He deserves the dignity of any man who does his duty. You will be counted when you return."

"Counted?" asked Olaf.

"wnmislwe?" added Bohai.

The young captain of the Nautilus looked down at the body of his helmsman; his expression of loss and compassion was real. "Regrettably, there will now be *two* funerals in the morning with the rising of the sun. But we *will* find their murderer. For whoever is *missing*," said Dakkar, scanning the handful of ship's crew on hand, "*is* the 'beast'. Strip the flesh from this 'werewolf' and we'll find nothing more than a sheep underneath, eh, Herr Henny?"

Henny arched a shoulder to indicate his ignorance, raised his right hand, palm up, and asked, "Couldn't the werewolf *hide*, Cap'n? The Nautilus is full of possible places to hide, yah."

"From the moon?" asked Dakkar. "Hide from the moon, Herr Henny? When everyone is on deck, how will the werewolf hide from the light of the moon? I don't think there will be time for our monster to *shave* his entire body."

Rajesh Dakkar turned from the Prussian to approach the two Chops.

"Chop, where are *your* bloody claws?" asked Dakkar of the China man nicknamed Lamb. He turned to watch Henny's response.

"Hck?!" was the gurgled answer he received as Lamb presented his hands for all to see.

"Chop," continued Dakkar as he stepped before the second China man, "do I smell helmsman on *your* breath?"

"Derk," was the gurgled denial from Bohai as he held his own hands up in front of his face.

Both of the China men saluted the captain as Dakkar stepped away from them.

As he stopped by Singh's side, Rajesh Dakkar watched the rest of his ship's crew gathering in a loose line on deck, their expressions ranging from indifference to guarded suspicion, to bewilderment. As they did so, Andrew covered his mouth and leaned close to Rajesh's left ear. He whispered, "Lamb and zee Pork. Why do they never answer?"

"Tongues," whispered Dakkar with a mischievous smile. "Their Emperor cut out their tongues for mangling their language. Now, back in line, my French friend."

Andrew straightened at the statement, disbelief apparent on his face. "I think my loyal service could earn me the simple, straightforward answer *once in awhile*, Captain," he said.

Rajesh smiled as he began to count the sailors with a bobbing finger. "Just count, my dear friend. One, two, three. You *have* my respect. I just regret that I haven't been able to invent a *sense of humor* for you yet."

"That's the kettle calling the pot black, eh, Captain?"

As one, the two Chops covered their mouths with their hands to hide their snickering.

With dedication overcoming his disbelief, Singh carefully counted the crew with Rajesh, excluding the expeditionary crew, and announced, "All are accounted for, Captain Dakkar. The number of ship's crew exactly matches the number who boarded the Nautilus when we set sail, my Lord."

"And not a fang in sight," smiled Rajesh Dakkar. He took a moment to make his point visually by sharing that smile, one at time, with Henny, Legrand, Templeton, and both of the Chops. "And, once again, I am proven right!"

"I believe you have proven nothing with zee certainty, Captain," said Andrew.

"Andrew! Surely you understand that the moon *proves* our murderer in no monster. If it were one of these," he continued, sweeping his hand to indicate all of the crew on deck, "someone would surely be howling at it about now. And to further prove the strength of my belief, *I* shall patrol tonight, *alone*, to secure the lives of everyone on this ship. Now, back to your stations, sirs."

Indra leaned close to Dakkar's ear as the men began to return to their stations or their cabins. He whispered, "Alone, sahib?!? Alone? You completely dismiss even the possibility of this beast *simply* because no crew member was missing?"

"No, my friend," responded Rajesh. "For the reasons just mentioned and one other."

"Because there was one too many."

Chapter Nine

The full moon hung directly over the sleeping Nautilus as the brig gently rose and fell on the Mediterranean like the shallow breath of a sleeping man. It was barely a silhouette against the star splashed midnight sky above and the inky waves below and around the ship. No sound came from below deck; not even the gurgle of the ship's boiler; stoked just enough to keep its fire from going out. As soft as a sigh, the mournful, metallic twang of a sitar barely disturbed the night's deep silence as its notes drifted from the brig across the waves.

Dakkar sat against a barrel, out of uniform, his left leg raised with that foot flat on the deck, and his right leg stretched before him. His sitar was nestled across his right hip and his stomach as he strummed its complex of strings. He seemed lost in a revere as he softly sang to the somber chords:

♪What do you do with a drunken sailor,
What do you do with a drunken sailor,
What do you do with a drunken sailor?

Early in the morning!
Way hay and up she rises,
Way hay and up she rises,
Way hay and up she rises,
Early in the morning.
Shave his belly with a rusty razor,
Shave his belly with a rusty razor,
Shave his belly with a rusty razor,
Early in the morning!♫

He smiled to himself at his inappropriate choice of raucous lyrics for such a somber occasion, and at his own rebellious nature against anything traditional or expected by the average man. As its chords slowly faded, the captain arched his left eyebrow and scanned the deck from left to right for a sound possibly imagined. Satisfied that there was nothing audible, Rajesh Dakkar rose from the deck to lean against the gunwale of the Nautilus, his forearms on the damp railing.

"Enough of that," he said to no one but himself. "Someday, I must learn to play something more dignified like the pipe organ."

He carefully leaned his sitar against the hull. He placed both of his hands on the rail and, for long moments of self-reflection, stared at the vast expanse of the black ocean that stretched beyond sight into the infinity of night. It was as abstract concept of infinity; he had to admit to himself that was impossible to prove through science. He would certainly never mention that to Singh.

The low growl behind him sounded like ratcheting gears.

Without turning , Rajesh said, "You are late."

He turned.

It snarled, baring its rabid, slobbering fangs; the claws of its raised hands threatened death.

Those fangs and claws were yellow and razor-sharp. Its humanoid body with the head of a wolf crouched on its back legs, all yellow, burning, feral eyes, and wire-haired fury. Its hot breath stank of blood; its hair was dirty and matted. Simultaneously, Rajesh fell to his left knee and drew out a vicious, long bladed knife.

The ravenous werewolf roared and leapt.

Dakkar only had time to whisper, "Roar?"

In one movement, Dakkar rose and slashed his knife in a wide arc before him, but missed the beast as the werewolf jerked back.

The monster slapped the knife from Dakkar's hand.

...the claws of its raised hands threatened death.

Rajesh Dakkar spat, "Damn."

The responding growl was ratcheting gears.

Dakkar turned to the sitar leaning against the railing and snatched it up. He grunted, as he swung it in a wide arc like a club.

Effortlessly, the werewolf side-stepped the arc of the sitar. The instrument smashed against the railing in an explosion of shards and frets and strings behind Dakkar.

Clawed hands seized Dakkar by the throat, creating bloody puncture wounds at the point of each claw, and slammed him back hard against the side of the gunwale. Face to face with Rajesh, the slavering beast screamed, its claws deep in Rajesh's throat, shaking and choking the life out of him.

Struggling to remain conscious and alive, Dakkar's left hand desperately, blindly clawed the air, searching for the werewolf's face or throat, but found instead the monster's scalp. His fingers embedded in the matted fur there and he yanked up.

Rajesh held the werewolf's hairy head, oddly like a deflated balloon, in his left hand. For a second, the image did not register on his fading sight.

The third eye painted on the forehead beneath the werewolf mask could not produce the same startled, murderous emotion as the two very human eyes of Rajesh's now unmasked assailant. The thug's hairy, gloved right hand, embedded at each fingertip with razor-sharp, iron spikes, released the Prince's throat, drew back slightly, and slowly descended again to rip out Dakkar's eyes.

The thug snarled, "Who's...late...NOW! You...Indian...bas..."

Bang!

"...tard." The word died as a bloody red hole was punched beneath his painted third eye.

The werewolf fell sideways, dead, to the deck.

"Dakkar!" Singh called out. He ran to his captain, kneeling on one knee by the corpse laying face down at his captain's feet. "Thank God, you're alive!"

Trembling, Rajesh rose up. Partially supporting his weight with his right hand on the railing, he looked down at the corpse, now looking ridiculously like a dirty hair rug instead of a supernatural horror. He placed his free hand on his neck, took it away, and looked at the blood smeared on his palm. He tried a nervous laugh, but failed and coughed instead.

"Why, Singh, you old liar," he said weakly, and placed the thumb of his right hand on his cheek, cupping his remaining fingers on his chin "You disobeyed my orders. I told you to stay below deck."

Dakkar stood, unsteady, by the corpse of the bloody horror as Indra Singh knelt by it, rolling it over to see the dead man's face.

"A wise man," he said, "never gambles with a fool's life, sahib."

"You speak in a paradox? A *fool's* life, Singh? Surely you can't mean me, because *this* wise man never gambles. *You* must certainly agree with me, Herr Henny?"

With his Pottsdam musket held diagonally from his left hip across his chest, Henny walked with pride to the side of his captain. The Prussian stopped to look down at his victim on the deck.

"Donnervetter! You were right! This is no werewolf?!?"

"I have never seen this man," added Singh.

"Yes, Henny, no werewolf, as your excellent shot helped me prove. But, Herr Henny...did you even for a moment doubt me?"

"Ja. I did. And it cost me a *silver* bullet."

"Where on earth did you get a silver bullet, Mr. Lagle?" asked Rajesh as he again knelt by the corpse next to Singh and raised the man's head using his left hand.

"*Now* who's got no humor! Just joking," smiled Henny slapping his right thigh for emphasis. "I had got no silver bullet, captain."

With his free hand, Rajesh pointed at the third eye just above the bloody hole in the man's forehead as Andrew joined them.

"This was a Soter assassin."

"What is a 'Soter.'" asked the Frenchman.

"When I counted the crew last night, it was *he* that numbered *one too many*. He must have been a stowaway. In addition to the superstitious nonsense, the 'beast' was a fake because that count of my men *under the moon* proved the 'werewolf' was a spy who could remove a disguise to rejoin the crew without being discovered."

"M'sieu Dakkar, he is a spy?!?" asked Andrew. "Oui?"

"Yes, M'sieu Andrew," responded the captain as he rose again from the body. "The time for secret destinations and hidden purposes is past, now."

Dakkar placed his fists on his hips, leaned back slightly at the waist, tossed his head slightly back, and smiled with the enthusiasm and optimism only possible in the young. "We are going digging, sirs. In Egypt's sands, digging for fire.

"We are going to Atlantis."

"Atlantis," sneered Olaf, contemptuously "I think it blows pretty soon and pretty hard!"

"Olaf!" scolded Singh. "Your oath!?"

"See," the dwarf grinned sheepishly, "I told you it will blow."

At that moment and deep beneath the ancient city of Alexandria, Egypt, four hooded and robed acolytes followed by a man wearing a pith helmet, long-sleeved jacket, and jodhpurs carefully descended the rough-hewn, treacherous steps that spilled out of the black mouth of a tunnel behind them and snaked down into a massive and dimly-lit cavern. The faces of the four acolytes were obscured by their hoods. The face of their guest was not hidden. It was full of fear and excitement.

The air was hot, stagnant, and oppressive. The tunnel behind them and the cavern before them were claustrophobic. The man in the pith helmet was an Englishman and an inveterate explorer whose blond, walrus mustache swept back and blended with bushy sideburns. He was dirty and exhausted from the long trek through the confusing maze of passageways now above them, but he said nothing as the men continued to descend. The muffled footfalls of five sets of leather boots with the distant *plop plip plop plip plop plip* of unseen water dripping from jagged clusters of stalactites echoed in his ears and disturbed the otherwise eerie silence. He smiled involuntarily. The sounds were somewhat of a comfort for the Englishman's overtaxed nerves.

He wiped stinging sweat from his bushy eyebrows and eyes with the heels of his hands and refused to look at the massive bas-relief chiseled from the wall on his left side. The gigantic face there was too much, too great a challenge to his sense of reality, and only the passion to hold the object of his obsession in his hands after decades of longing overcame his fear and drove him on.

Three of the four hooded men plodding in front of the Englishman carried flickering torches in their raised left hands that threw dancing shadows on the damp cavern walls. Dependent on that light, the Englishman kept close to the nearest acolyte as they finally stepped onto the floor of the cavern. It was more obvious now that the monstrous relief, eighteen feet high and ten feet wide, was the graven image of the face of the Roman god, Zeus, his dead, pupil-less eyes fixed on eternity.

The English explorer still refused to even glance at the monstrous visage except from the corner of his eye as the first of the four acolytes disappeared into the black maw of another tunnel opposite Zeus' image. His anticipation has now reached its peak; his hands were shaking slightly.

The explorer removed his helmet and ran his trembling left hand through his blond hair matted with sweat, then replaced his headgear as the last of the hooded men entered the tunnel.

He entered as well, and immediately stumbled. He threw out his left hand against the tunnel's damp wall to save himself from falling, and looked down to see what had tripped him.

There was nothing but the floor.

He looked up as the fourth acolyte disappeared around a turn in the tunnel, taking the light from his torch with him. The Englishman glanced to his right a second before that light disappeared.

He gasped.

In a niche cut out of the wall opposite him, he saw the bleached skeleton, stitched together with golden wire, of a centaur galloping without moving. Its human skull was a hideous repudiation of all that the Englishman believed. He saw, and then the image was stolen away with the light.

Breathless, the Englishman whispered, "Wait..." and, pressing his body hard against the wall, rapidly inched his away down the tunnel until the horror of the impossible was replaced with the receding back of the fourth hooded man carrying the sanity saving torch.

Again, he whispered "Wait," but his guides were too far ahead of him to hear his frantic plea.

The unblinking, painted third eye with the oozing red hole beneath it stared up at Dakkar who stood over the faux werewolf on the deck of the Nautilus, indifferent to the horror of death at his feet. He gauged the emotions on the faces of Andrew, Olaf, Singh, Henny and the Chops as he spoke.

"Listen, Andrew, and learn," he continued. "The Ptolemaic kings, successors of Alexander the Great who had conquered most of the known world, set a staggering goal for themselves. They were probably inspired by Alexander's own insatiable thirst for knowledge. Even before 285 B.C., Ptolemy I, called 'Soter' or 'Savior', directed that all the books ever written as well as the marvels of antiquity should be gathered and stored in a library."

"This library and museum built in Alexandria, Egypt, would stand for over 925 years. Imagine what must have been gathered over nine centuries. But with time, delicate scrolls, most translated into Greek, were replaced by parchment and bound. Most were translated into Greek; only the rarest scrolls were preserved in their original tongues."

Dakkar saw that his expeditionary crew was riveted on his every word. He finished with, "It ultimately held 700,000 scrolls and unnumbered objects that many believed were only legend and myth."

The final echo of their footfalls faded into silence as the Englishman and his four faceless guides stopped in front of arched, ivory paneled, double doors blocking the tunnel. Torches were mounted in the walls. The doors were hung between two Corinthian columns under an elongated, marble panel adorned with eldritch Egyptian cartouches. The acolyte without a torch approached the left door, grabbed a golden ring embedded on its right side, and pushed. The huge door slowly swung in and, as they entered, his four hooded guides separated into two groups of two men on either side of the explorer. Puzzled, the Englishman stopped and glanced at the robed men to his left and right sides as the two nearest the door stepped back and partially behind him.

He licked his lips. Then he looked ten paces inside and ahead of himself into a tiled room. The explorer's open hands were instinctively crossed in reverence in front of his chest, and awe and surprise drew an open-mouthed smile on his face.

"Oh my God," he gasped. "It *is* real, real!"

His words hung in the smarmy air in the otherwise uncanny silence of the ancient tomb.

The Englishman and his guides moved reverently across the threshold and into the outre room.

The four acolytes stopped first and turned their backs to the Englishman to face the door through which they had entered.

The English explorer stopped, inspired by two magnificent, golden braziers against the opposite wall that face him standing in the center of the area paneled with exquisite, veined, marble panels. Their bronze bowels flickered with fire atop thin, marble stands taller than any man. He dropped his crossed hands to his sides. He drew an unnaturally deep breath. As he did so, wild shadows danced in the tomb, distorting everything they touched.

These priceless braziers, in turn, were flanked by two thick, marble columns that rose from floor to ceiling. Between those columns and braziers stood an exquisite pedestal chiseled from a single, perfect slab of marble. Preternatural half-human creatures cavorted around its stand.

Draped over the top of that altar was the radiant, yellow, tightly curled fleece and gilded, doubly-twisted horns of a splendid, abnormally large ram.

His trembling right hand outstretched to touch it, the Englishman drew near the glowing fleece.

"Th-the Golden Fleece!" he whispered. "All m-my life…"

He touched it.

The fleece slipped off the pedestal and fell to the floor.

In its place on the stand lay a scaly, dead horror of vacant eyes, razor teeth, forked tongue, and frozen screams caught forever in an idiot's gaping mouth. The hideous thing lay on the pedestal in a pool of ancient, clotted, black blood that still fringed its neck where its head had been severed from its body long before the first brick of Rome had ever been raised.

The dead, frigid snakes on its head writhed like maggots and struck without movement.

It was Medusa that forever leered in the rigors of death, and the Englishman threw up his arms in front of his face in an utterly vain attempt to defend himself as the blood in his veins began to calcify, his heart spasmed and stopped, the organs in his body turned to dust and mummification, his skin blistered, cracked, and hardened, and living flesh became dead stone.

Their backs to the monster on the pedestal, and one by one, the four acolytes pushed their hoods back off of their faces. Not a word was spoken.

The painted third eye of a Soter was painted in the center of each forehead.

The unblinking third eye of Horus and the oozing red hole in the forehead of the pseudo-werewolf stared up at Dakkar who studied the expressions of Andrew, Olaf, Singh, Henny and the Chops as he finished his story.

"Eventually, Greek priests now called Soters were given charge of these priceless and unique treasures. They were a small and secret cult sworn to maintain and protect the contents of the library with their lives. Indeed, many Soters died doing just so as thieves, conquering armies, and even their own jaded rulers, depleted or damaged the library over the centuries.

"In 640 A. D., the unthinkable happened and a horde of Arabs conquered Egypt. And when Alexandria fell and Caliph Omar was asked what to do with the library, the greatest collection of knowledge in the world, he decreed: 'As for the books you mention, here is my reply. If their content is in accordance with the Koran, we may do without them. For, in that case, the Koran more than suffices. If, on the other hand, they contain matter not in accordance with the Koran...there can be no need to preserve them. Destroy them'.

"Seven hundred thousand volumes were burned to heat the bath houses of Alexandria as Omar's army washed away the filth, blood, and shame of war. Or so thought the Arabs and the world. But, anticipating the eventuality of conquest by an outside force, and by centuries of hidden toil, the Soter cult had secretly enlarged natural, subterranean grottoes, tunnels, and caverns that honeycombed the earth beneath the library. And throughout the centuries, they had duplicated the library's books and artifacts. The copies they placed in the museum above ground. But the glorious originals were hidden in the caverns below."

"Gentlemen, the library and museum exist to this day."

Dakkar looked down at the face framed by the long, black, matted hair of the dead Soter assassin. The werewolf mask lay crumpled into a ball of fur by his left ear. The red hole had wept blood down his forehead and onto the deck of the Nautilus until his heart had stopped pumping.

"And inside the Library," Dakkar continued, "are the last extant Atlantean writings. Inside those scrolls lies the secret I seek, gentlemen. The daughter of Nechops, the chief Soter, believed her father wrong to withhold the vast knowledge stored in that subterranean library from the world. She stole the map to the hidden library that I bought in Delhi, and that will lead us to the treasure I seek.

"Nechops struggled to stop her from selling it to me in Delhi. And, when that failed, this 'werewolf' was sent to retrieve the map at any cost. Their second attempt to do so lies dead at our feet. Their spy did not stop me. Nothing will stop me, sirs, until the Atlantean scroll gives up its secret and in my hands I hold...the thunderbolts of Jove!"

"And what proof do you have, Captain Dakkar, that this map is not a fake?" asked Andrew.

"None," said Dakkar. "Well know when we arrive."

With the backs of their left hands on their foreheads, Chop and Chop puffed up their cheeks, then expelled their breath to express their endurance of Dakkar's long speech. As they did so, crewmen Michael and Robert arrived with a rolled up linen sheet to cover the Soter's corpse. Henny, touching his temple as if he had a headache, shook his head and simply walked away.

Rajesh said, "Today, double tragedy, Singh. The death of any man is a tragedy. But tomorrow...tomorrow this rough-hewn gaggle of pickpockets, mercenaries, cuckolds and cutthroats become my 'Black Knights.'"

"The thunderbolts of Zeus in your hand, Dakkar?" interrupted Andrew. "It is impossible."

"No, M'sieu Andrew. What can be done will be done, and I am 'zee' man to do it."

"God forbid, sahib," said Singh, swabbing his bald pate from front to back with his right hand. "I fear that for *only* good to come from your belief, my prince, it would be necessary for either evil to not exist or for the world to be morally neutral, and neither thing it true."

"Yap, yap, yap," said the dwarf, pulling his ear with his left hand. "The only thing I know for certain is I'm a dead man,"

Chapter Ten

The gibbous yellow sun at the horizon of the Mediterranean welcomed a new day as it hung in a cerulean blue sky above the Nautilus. A small flock of seagulls circled the brig like cinders rising above a fire and without the aid of even the slightest of breezes as Rajesh's Black Knights rose, one by one, in their rooms below deck. That slowly rotating ring of sea birds implied that land was near.

Because there was no breeze, deep below the deck at the Nautilus' stern, water churned inside the ship's huge, gurgling boiler that huffed and clanked and huffed again. Heavily muscled crewmen striped to their waists rhythmically stoked black coal into its belly.

Unseen, the water inside heated by the burning coal violently boiled into steam that screamed out of the boiler and through the large copper tube welded to the boiler's super-heated belly. The steam roared through the tube under great pressure to interconnected gears that lifted levers that opened or shut values that lifted or set, moved or stopped innumerable hidden mechanisms leading to pistons. Those pistons pumped up and down and up and down and turned the axle that spun the massive screw in furious motion below the ship's stern outside and thrust the brig through the relatively cold waters of the ocean. The sweating men stoking the boiler were not the only ones concerned with the Nautilus' steam-driven engine that morning.

Chewing a toothpick, Rajesh leaned his left forearm on the starboard gunwale of the Nautilus. The young captain of his ship watched the long, horizontal snake of grey steam and smoke that was exhausted through the vent on the hull hang just above the moderate waves of the sea.

Rajesh was not without pride. He was, however, without humility. He shook his raven black hair and touched the red dot just above his grey eyes on the center of his forehead with the index finger of his right hand as, behind him, a voice interrupted his musings.

"The Shudra bindi on your forehead denotes the lowest Hindu caste of a laborer, artisan or servant, and is, therefore, atrociously improper for a *Prince* of India, my Lord. But, of course, you already know that. I just thought I'd remind you."

Rajesh straightened up from the gunwale and turned to face his mentor, Indra Singh. He took the toothpick from his mouth. "Ah, good morning, my friend and greatest critic. I didn't hear you approach. And am I not 'atrociously improper for a Prince of India' in all ways, Indra? Now that that's settled for all time, how can I make this beautiful morning even better for you?"

"Rub the bindi off of your forehead." Indra pressed his palms together at his chest in an attitude of prayer, and bowed slightly at the waist. "For all time."

"I will stop poking my finger in the eye of tradition and wipe it off when you add one to your forehead, Singh." Rajesh returned the toothpick to his mouth.

"But I am not a Hindu."

"Exactly my point. A Christian in Hindu India? I would say that we are both poking fingers in the eyes of tradition. But that doesn't concern me in the least. I am interested in facts and nothing else. Not man-made tradition, custom, religion or opinion. If I had my way, they would all disappear today. But since I have no way to make that happen, I will continue to sacrifice anything and everything, including your opinion of my inappropriate bindi, for truth."

"Anything and everything, sahib? You've already sacrificed three any one's," said Singh. "Are you so sure that isn't enough?"

The smile on Rajesh's young face vanished. "You have crossed the limits of our friendship with that foolish comment, Singh."

"Limits, my Prince? I wasn't aware our friendship had limits."

"Whether sentient life was created by a random act of nature, as I believe, or by a Creator God, as you believe, that doesn't change the fact one iota that I put the highest value on human life. Your words were meant to shame me. But you are wrong to do so. That I don't wear my compassion on my sleeve for those who died doesn't mean that I don't mourn their deaths. Our conversation is over, Singh. Go. Set up the demonstration table and prepare the tools that the expedition team will carry into the library. Then call my Black Knights on deck."

"As you wish, sahib." Indra Singh bowed his head submissively and walked away.

The captain of the Nautilus turned his back on his mentor and teacher, and again leaned his forearms on the gunwale.

"I am no ignorant child or fool," said Dakkar to the universe in the new silence broken only by the lapping of the waves against the Nautilus. 'As men, we are all equal in the face of death.'"

So saying, he took the toothpick from his mouth and tossed it into the sea.

Earlier that morning, the rising sun on the ocean's horizon had swum like a tiny glowing crystal ball between the first and second of three broad, wooden planks secured from the starboard gunwale to the tops of three barrels lashed to the deck of the Nautilus. On each plank had lain a long, tightly wrapped mummy; three beige cocoons of muslin hiding the nasty and indisputable evidence of human mortality. No strong, salt breeze repeatedly added and then erased folds from everything cloth, or ruffled the hair of the somber crew gathered on the deck. Everything had been uncannily still like a held breath.

Standing "at ease", Dakkar's expeditionary team and, behind them, the remaining crew of the Nautilus, had stood facing the planks. Singh, holding a small, open, black book in both hands, and Rajesh had stood at the right side of the planks. Rajesh, Singh, and the expeditionary team had all worn black, long-sleeved, pull-over shirts without buttons or pockets, beige, canvas pants, and black belts and boots; the uniform that Rajesh had designed for his "Black Knights". Only Olaf had worn a beret. The crew of the brig had worn their formal, blue, double-breasted uniforms.

"Gentlemen it is time." said Rajesh, "Atten-shon!"

Sounding like gunshots in the otherwise eerie silence, the entire crew had clicked the heels of their boots together and straightened in rigid, silent respect as Singh opened his black book.

"Aiguo and Bohai Chop," Rajesh had intoned, "man your station."

The two, twin China men had marched to the plank nearest them, and stopped, standing at attention.

"M'sieu Andrew Legrand; Mr. Olaf Templeton, man your post."

The Frenchman and the dwarf had marched to the middle plank and stopped, standing at attention as well. Olaf had sneezed once but did not raise a hand to squelch it.

"Herr Henny Lagle," Rajesh had added, and joined the Prussian as he marched to the far plank and stopped. Each of the two member teams had placed their hands under the end of the planks nearest them. From the ranks of the Nautilus' crew, one of the sailors had raised a brass bugle to his mouth and played four bars of a melancholy dirge on his instrument that only added to the uncanny atmosphere.

Henny had removed his left hand from the plank and wiped a tear from his right eye.

"Nature never promises justice," Rajesh had said. "So, this morning, we commemorate the unjust loss of two lives and the just but tragic loss of a third man. As the Roman, Seneca, wrote of death: 'A punishment to some, to some a gift, and to many a favor.'"

Singh had taken one step forward and stopped, opening his black book.

"We therefore commit each of these bodies to the deep," he had read from the book, "to be turned into corruption, looking for the resurrection of the body, when the Sea shall give up her dead, and the life of the world to come, through our Lord Jesus Christ; who at His coming shall change our vile body, that it may be like His glorious body, according to the mighty working, whereby He is able to subdue all things to Himself."

As one, the three teams of men then raised the ends of their planks; the cocoons slid one by one, first, the cook, then the helmsman, and finally the Soter assassin, down the boards, over the gunwale, and into the ocean. They had sunk beneath its waves.

"Amen, and amen," concluded Indra. "This ends this sacred ceremony."

"Amen," each of the Knights had said in a random pattern and with virtually no understanding of the words of the ceremony or of the word amen.

"Gentleman," Rajesh had said, "Life is for the living. We are dismissed."

The captain of the Nautilus shook the memory of the funeral that morning out of his head as he leaned his forearms on the starboard gunwale, watching the long, horizontal snake of grey steam and smoke hanging behind his ship just above the water. The sky was now spotted with a handful of cotton ball clouds, and a breeze now disturbed the curls of his raven hair, but not enough for him to order the sails unfurled. He straightened. To no one but himself he repeated: "'As men, we are all equal in the presence of death.'"

"More importantly, we are all equal in the eyes of God."

"What?" asked Rajesh as he tuned to face the unexpected author of the statement.

"I don't know who said or wrote it," said Singh as he reached his captain's side, "but I like: 'God pours life into death and death into life without a drop being spilled.'"

"Ah, Singh. An interesting thought, old friend. Are we ready?"

"As you instructed."

His mentor waved the open palm of his right hand to direct Rajesh's attention to a small, wooden table and the objects on it that stood several yards from them. Rajesh turned to look at the table and, behind it, his five hand-chosen men. "We are all ready."

"Ah, my Black Knights. At your ease," he said and pointed a finger at the table and the items on it as he and Singh approached it. "Gentlemen, these are the tools that I've anticipated we may need on our adventure together. And, as discussed with each of you before our meeting this morning, each of you will also demonstrate one or two of your own skills as well."

"Before you do that," interrupted the Frenchman, "I am curious, my captain. Why have you called us your 'Black Knights.'"

"It is simple, Mr. Legrand. I grew up reading and loving the adventures of King Arthur and his Round Table of knights, and the uniform you wear that I designed for you includes a black shirt. So please think of the name as nothing more than my whim."

Rajesh turned to the table that displayed a coil of rope, a Shepherd's Crook of about six feet in length, a disassembled musket, and an oddly shaped pistol. The captain picked up the coil of rope, found its end, and held it up for the crew to ascertain.

"Each of us will carry a fifteen foot coil of rope that is intertwined and therefore reinforced with a wire of my invention. These ropes have ten times the tensile strength of piano wire. We will wear it around our stomachs and under our shirts. As you can see, there is a catch and an eyelet at the end of each rope. Mr. Templeton, please help me demonstrate."

Grudgingly, Olaf walked to the table, turned to face his fellows, and pulled up his shirt. Around his waist was a coil of the rope above the belt he always wore of his pickpocket's tools. He unwound several loops of the rope and presented its end to his captain. Rajesh hooked the end of the rope he held to Olaf's line.

"These ropes, removed and latched together, will give us a single unit of one hundred and five feet in length. We may need them to ascend or descend otherwise un-scalable heights or depths that we may encounter in the library. There may be other uses for these ropes as well."

"Like to tie up the midget so he don't steal everything in sight," said Henny with a broad grin.

"Enough of that kind of insult, Henny. From this moment forward, we must be a team, each bringing his own skill to that team for the benefit of us all. One for all, all for one."

"Well done, Mr. Templeton," continued Dakkar as Olaf rolled his shirt back over the rope. "I think we all know what Mr. Templeton brings to the table."

"Wee. The ability to borrow monies from you without you knowing it," quipped the Frenchman.

"It is now M'sieu Andrew's turn," said Rajesh, ignoring the Frenchman's comment, "to demonstrate my Shepherd's Crook and his skill with it. Andrew?"

The Frenchman nodded as he approached the table, and picked up the crook. With a quick jerk, he separated the hook from the staff, revealing a long, lethal foil embedded inside it. Legrand assumed the standing position of a master swordsman.

"M'sieu Andrew," said Rajesh, "is among the greatest swordsmen in France."

"Non," said Andrew, and lunged, parried, riposted, fleched, and remised with an imaginary opponent. "I am the greatest swordsman in France, my friends, and the world!"

Instantly, Aiguo fell forward into the first of a series of three lightening somersaults, removing the cleaver under his shirt on his second flip. He landed at the side of Andrew's extended foil. Bohai, one second behind his brother, mimicked Lamb, arriving at the left side of the foil.

Andrew said, "What zee..." as Aiguo's cleaver swung down in a lightning fast arc and severed the point of the foil that dropped into Bohai's cupped and waiting palms.

Andrew's surprise soured.

"Azrgbed!" said Lamb.

"Meztred!" added Pork.

"Sacre bleu!" Andrew gasped, his eyes as large as bronze coins. "They are wraiths!"

"Indeed, M'sieu Andrew," said Rajesh. "The Chop twins were among the exclusive warriors who personally guarded the Emperor of China. You have seen only one of their hidden talents, and have earned the right to learn something more of our enigmatic twins. I know you have all wondered if they were born mute or some accident stole their ability to speak. The truth is this. To make sure no secret of the court was ever leaked, their Emperor had their tongues cut out."

"Damn!" Andrew exclaimed, his left hand instinctively on his own mouth.

"ut," repeated both of the China men, their left hands instinctively on their own mouths.

"Well done, Chops, although completely unplanned. Luckily, I have a second foil to replace the one you just destroyed. The cost of the foil you ruined will come out of your stipend."

Smiles faded from their faces as they dropped their hands from their mouths and returned to the ranks of their fellows.

"Our marksman, Herr Henny Lagle, is the next and final Black Knight to display his most impressive talent today. Henny?"

At his arrival at the table, the Prussian picked up the parts of the musket without hesitation and quickly assembled the weapon.

"Donnerveiter," he said, making no effort to hide an expression of surprise and curiosity. He easily twisted the barrel 180° until it snapped into a second per-engineered position. "I have not seen this before! This is a double barrel musket?!"

"Yes, Herr Lagle, a revolutionary rifle, indeed," he said, cupping the fingers of his right hand below his chin. "You will now be able to fire two shots before having to reload your weapon. You will wear it under your clothing attached by a special harness to your left leg. But the rifle is not what I wish you to demonstrate today. Please pick up the pistol on the table. Each of us will carry one on our adventure with four preloaded barrels."

Henny picked up the pistol and slowly and carefully turned it over in his big hands as he examined it.

"What Herr Henny Lagel is studying and that you cannot see is that I have re-engineered the traditional pistol that uses gun power and shot. My pistol has a barrel with four cylinders behind and below the barrel. Without reloading, it will allow a person to rapidly discharge four projectiles, not one, and fires a dart tipped with a chemical that almost instantly paralyzes its victim."

"Like one of Olaf's love stories of the bearded lady," said Henny as he balanced the weight of the pistol in his right hand. "Yah, little one?"

"In addition," continued Rajesh, "its grip is actually made of a very thick glass coated inside with asbestos. It is charged with steam from the Nautilus' boiler under incredible pressure. When Henny pulls the trigger, a tiny, concentrated blast of the superheated steam will hurl a dart effectively up to fifty yards away. Herr Henny, show us how it works. Do you think you can hit Mr. Templeton's beret as he holds it against the main mast?"

"What the hell!" the dwarf objected.

"To the mast now, Mr. Templeton," said Rajesh without emotion.

"When you kiss my lily white a..."

Aiguo shoved the dwarf towards the mast.

"Hey, get your yellow paw off of me," growled the dwarf as he turned to face the China man who was quietly patting the dull side of the blade of his cleaver into the palm of his left hand.

The blood drained from Olaf's face. "You let him push me around like that?" he asked of Rajesh.

"You have nothing to fear, Mr. Templeton. Herr Henny can easily shoot the eye out of a gnat at fifty feet."

Reluctantly, and with the blood flushing his face red, Olaf removed his beret and, holding his hand out at arm's length, placed his beret against the mast.

Extending Dakkar's steam pistol in his right hand and sighting carefully along its barrel, Henny said, "Done und done, captain."

He pulled the trigger of the steam-charged pistol. The pistol barked. A dart *thip* was embedded near the center of Olaf's cap. With the exception of Dakkar, Henny, and Olaf (who audibly swallowed hard) the Black Knights gasped.

Henny smiled and sighted carefully along the barrel of the pistol. He pulled the trigger a second time. The second missile *thip* embedded in Olaf's beret only inches away from the first dart.

"Good," Henny said, and pulled the trigger again. The gun exploded in a cloud of steam, blasting his sideburns, mustache, and hair back like a blown dandelion and scalding his face and hand. Cursing, he dropped the pistol to the deck.

"Damn!" exclaimed Rajesh. "It failed!"

"Sacre bleu," whispered Andrew.

"galpt!" added Aiguo.

Olaf wet his pants.

Chapter Eleven

Diary of the Nautilus. 1884. Lincoln Island. Dakkar Grotto. South Pacific.

"We docked before sunrise in the Alexandrian harbor where Caesar had fought desperately for his life centuries earlier. He succeeded. I had no doubt that I would do so as well. Logic demanded every thought be focused on unemotional, detached observation. But my heart leapt as I and my Black Knights disembarked from the Nautilus

He pulled the trigger…the pistol barked.

because I knew that, buried at my feet in immense, forgotten caverns,
there lay the remnants of Atlantean science...and the secret of a fire
that does not consume."

The dusty, narrow, flagstone road that Dakkar and his Black Knights traveled after leaving their brig snaked up, over, and then down the landward side of a small hill overlooking the bay where the Nautilus was docked. Centuries ago, the Lighthouse of Alexandria had towered over that harbor and the ancient city. In its long descent on the landward side, that road, more an alley than a street, twisted past a small, mulch-columned temple fallen out of use and into disrepair down into the center of a dirty, derelict ghetto of mostly two story buildings built of sun-baked brick on the outskirts of the Egyptian metropolis. The day was new; the street was sparsely populated.

A relentless yellow-red sun beat down on the seven Black Knights as they cautiously strolled between a cluster of grimy, pestilential tenements and businesses that flanked both sides of the road. Its relentless heat painted half-moons of sweat at their armpits and a smear of perspiration at their spines that were, for the most part, hidden by their black shirts. Except for the Chops, who both wore knapsacks filled with emergency medical supplies and canned food, all wore the uniform designed by their captain. They were clothed in the same outfits that they always wore. Andrew's only accessory was Dakkar's crook with its hidden foil that he was using as a walking stick.

"This is Egypt's best?" grumbled Olaf as he slapped a pest on the back of his neck. "The worst side-show I starred in played in better than this."

"Oui. I'm sure that's true, Olaf," said Andrew. "And that slap on your neck was the most applause you ever got, too."

Around them, a handful of poverty stricken men and women in dirty, tattered robes traveled to destinations unknown to Rajesh's men, sidestepping the garbage and slop that had been thrown from second story windows. Some shopped for household items or food, or lounged in doorways, or begged for alms sitting cross-legged in the heat. The old men and women of Alexandria sat on rickety chairs next to shop entrances, chatting about happier days. They all completely ignored the Black Knights.

"...simple prejudice..." pontificated Rajesh to Aiguo as they walked together, "that all our fore-bearers were ignorant savages, Chop." He and Aiguo watched a mongrel bitch tear at a scrap of something dead on the flagstone street. "Don't believe everything you hear. It simply is not true. You must learn to give the past its due."

"jekw," nodded Lamb who walked next to his brother and Singh. To the right of Indra, Andrew glanced at an effeminate man leaning against the jamb of an open door. His hand on his hip, and his right shoulder and leg bare, he winked at the Frenchman as Andrew drew near.

Legrand shook his head from side to side and raised his hands, palm out, to decline the blatant invitation. "Wrong gender, my friend. Sacre, for one night of pleasure among a thousand and one nights of delight!" he added with a sigh.

"And a thousand and two diseases," said Singh, shaking his own head in disapproval.

Of the seven adventurers, only Henny and Olaf stopped at a table created by pushing a large wooden section of a building's wall out and down in a horizontal position. The table was supported by rope tied from its extreme corners and fastened to the wall.

Seven, cheap oil lamps were displayed on the table as well as a small, cloth bag near the shop's mostly bald and fully bearded owner. He wore his robe open over a cotton undershirt with its two ends tucked into a cloth belt. The shopkeeper braced his right hand on the table while presenting one of his lamps with his left hand to potential customers as they passed him. Behind him, a tattered, red cotton curtain hung from ceiling to floor, dividing the merchant's home from his business.

The Prussian picked up one of the many oil lamps. He turned it over in his big hands.

"Donnervetter! This is not barter. This is robbery!" Lagle protested. "This is tin!"

"No, no, no. It is a bargain, guaranteed!" objected the shopkeeper with an oily smile. As he clutched the robe at the level of his chest, he beamed with pride, and claimed, "As Allah is my witness, some, indeed, are priceless because in every third lamp lives a Genie!"

"Highway robbery," added Olaf, removing his red beret. He wiped his forehead with the back of his hand, then returning the cap to his head. "It is a shame Dakkar's steam gun didn't work now. We could really clean up this joint! Hehehehe."

The laughter rang false.

"Shut up, Olaf," said the Prussian. He picked up one of the lamps and held it level with his eyes.

"I will give you half of your asking price," Henny said. "My final offer."

"Allah Akbar," the merchant said and slapped both of his cheeks with the palms of his hands. "Now who is the highway robber!"

"I think it will blow pretty soon, pretty hard here!" added the dwarf, winking his right eye and pulling his ear with his left hand. "Don't be a fool, well, er, at least this time, Herr Henny."

"And could you ever possibly stop saying that, you little gutter rat," snarled Henny. "It is irritating beyond belief!"

"In my country," continued the Prussian, "this piece of tin would be junk."

"Effendi," answered the merchant with faked injury to his integrity, "this lamp is made of Egypt's finest silver!"

Henny tossed back his head and placed his right hand at the nape of his neck as if addressing an invisible senate of his peers. "We make toy whistles of such 'silver' in Prussia."

The merchant leaned forward, gesturing wildly with animated hands, and earnestly objected, his attention fully focused on the marksman. "Good sir! I must object. My good name of Orosius is beyond question in Egypt. But, I, my wife, and my five little ones must eat, so I forgive your insult. You drive a hard bargain, but I'm old and hungry."

As the two bartered, grinning and pretending to be engaged in their lively debate, Templeton snatched the shopkeeper's cloth bag from among the oil lamps and stuffed it into his waistband at the small of his back.

"Do not make some noise," Olaf smirked at the shopkeeper, "but you are an old thief!"

"Jawohl, Mr. Templeton. An old thief and a new pauper." Henny presented his hand, palm open, to the shopkeeper, indicating he was finished debating. "No sale," he said as he turned away to leave. "My friend and I are finished here. Let's go, Olaf. I have been offended."

In two quick steps, Rajnesh was behind both men only to stumble against Olaf's back as he snatched the shopkeeper's bag from the dwarf's waistband.

As he did so, Rajesh said, "Oh, so sorry, Mr. Templeton. So clumsy of me. Please...proceed on your way. I'll catch up with you in a minute."

"Hey!" Olaf stopped, turned, and faced his captain with open suspicion. "If I don't know better....." he shook his head to dismiss his hunch. "No. No. You are excused, captain. Come, Herr Henny." So saying, Olaf rejoined the Prussian who had paused several feet away to watch the altercation between the dwarf and Rajesh.

"Old Orosius, the fool," Olaf groused, "will soon be parted with his money, eh, Henny?"

"Ja, ja. He don't see a thing. Good job and good practice for our little withdrawal later on from the library, eh, Mr. Templeton?"

As they walked away, Rajesh stood before the shopkeeper's table, waving the cloth bag in front of the vendor's surprised and grateful face.

"I think the genie in your lamp must have hopped into your bag and took himself a little trip," he said, "A wise man never tempts the virtue of his brother. Your purse, sir."

"Praise Allah! You will be richly rewarded not only here, but in the afterlife, effendi!"

"Tell your brothers to lock up their treasures. There are thieves abroad."

The vendor bowed and said, "Thank you, thank you, thank you, effendi!"

As Rajesh turned and walked away, he muttered, "Enjoy your reward now, Prince Dakkar. The afterlife comes more quickly for some than for others."

The shopkeeper eyes narrowed to crafty slits that never left Rajesh's back as Dakkar walked away. After enough moments to be sure that the young Indian was gone, the shop owner turned and disappeared through the curtain behind him.

Legrand leaned against the brick wall of a house with his right crossed over his left leg. His right seal skin boot lay on the flagstone road by his left leg as he vigorously rubbed his socked foot with both hands and grimaced.

"My feet are killing me, no?!" the Frenchman groused as the Chops, Dakkar, and Singh waited patiently for him to finish his chore. "Have we been on this road for hours or what?"

"A little over one hour," offered Rajesh. "Oddly enough, we all wear the same boots, and no one else complains of sore feet, sir."

"And all this to march into a horde of Soters and certain death."

"Ah, so that's the real reason for the delay. If by a horde you mean seven or eight terrifying librarians who are so brave and skilled that they hire henchmen to do their dirty work, M'sieu Andrew, then I suppose you are right. My suspicion is that our werewolf was a hired assassin, not a Soter."

"I pray that you are right, sahib," said Singh. "I still believe that the treasure you seek can add nothing to your family's already incredible wealth. But, then, how can I or any one of your Black Knights know for sure, since you still talk about it in riddles."

"As I have said before, Singh, we will bring the secret of this incredible power to the lives of millions and millions of men," said Dakkar. "And all will benefit. Can't you exercise some of that faith for which you are so famous and stop asking?"

"Bring? Is not the proper word 'steal'?," Singh objected. "When you 'bring' what you do not own, it is theft, sahib."

"And who owns fire? The Atlanteans who no longer exist? The Egyptians? According to your belief, if I steal, it must be from your God, the God who created fire. I, on the other hand, believe I take the secret of a fire that is elementary to nature. Either way, I take what the Soter's do not own. You, on the other hand mistake the truth of men for ultimate truth, old tutor."

As his captain and Indra argued, Olaf halted by a cart carrying a mound straw five yards behind them and grabbed Henny's shirt sleeve, dragging him to a stop as well. The dwarf slyly glanced to his right and left to see if he were watched before he whispered, "Stop, Henny, stop. This place be as good as any. Time to divvies up."

Twisting his body around as far as possible, Olaf reached for the bag he had stolen only to find nothing tucked in the waistband of his trousers at the small of his back.

"Godt in heaven!" he snorted, "It's gone!"

"What is gone," asked Henny. "Not the money bag?!?"

"Ya, ya, ya, just that. But what could of happ..." His eyes narrowed to cunning slits of fire as he remember Rajesh stumbling against him.

"Rajesh!" he hissed. "Why that....he'll live to regret the day I was born."

Henny shrugged his shoulders and raised his hands, palm up, to indicate ignorance.

"By gar, Olaf, as far as concerns you, I think he already do," he grinned.

Two rows of pitted and ancient Corinthian and Doric columns, three times the height of a man, adorned the face of the great stone building covered with Egyptian cartouches that faced the seven Black Knights. Two spread wings that emblazoned a single marble panel above a large, black door and set between two Doric columns silently announced the building's entrance. More than one cripple begged for a scarp of food or a coin on the worn steps leading to that door, and a handful of Arabic men and women moiled in front of the outer images of crocodile, falcon, and wolf-headed gods that embellished its once spectacular, but now stained and deteriorating, walls. Its final ornament was the feces of stray dogs, feral cats, and hordes of dirty pigeons.

"Knowledge belongs to all," said Rajesh, his arms raised as if in greeting. "Not the few who hoard what now lies below our feet. Behold...the Library of Alexandria!"

"Is this some kind of joke?" asked Andrew, scratching his head.

"Then the joke is on us," the dwarf responded as he pulled at his left ear.

"Well sahib," said Indra, looking up at the huge, decaying building, "is it possible that we are both deceived by 'truth'. The plaque on this building translates: 'Institution for the Criminally Insane.'"

"Singh! Have you forgotten I read this language as well as you? Did you expect it to say 'welcome, Dakkar; X marks the spot.'"

"Not that, Rajesh, but I didn't expect it to look like a garbage heap either."

To the left of the insane asylum was a marble panel decorated with a scene of Horus, the falcon-headed god, offering an object to a seated Pharaoh. His Queen stood behind him.

A turbaned beggar with a bowl in his hands and his mongrel dog were hunched in front of the panel like knotted desperation, and above it were a row of dirty, multi-paned windows. A pair of pigeons outside the windows above the marble panel were pecking at insects.

None of the seven Black Knights could hear the heated conversation behind one of the windows that was muffled by distance and glass.

"So," said the head of the institute as he stood gazing at the pigeons outside of the window, his hands intertwined behind his back. "You are caught sucking at the poppy again, Ptah. Apparently, your insatiable appetite is stronger than my threats."

The institute's director wore a light beige shirt open at the chest over a cotton undershirt, and cotton trousers. His matted black hair fell back from his partially bald head to his shoulders, with streaks of grey over each ear, and his black eyes sparkled like black onyx as he inveighed against Ptah.

"No," protested Ptah, the middle-aged, black bearded, and curly headed man who faced his accuser. "Nothing of the sort."

"And what, then, heals the melancholy eating at your soul that now drives you to the edge of madness and beyond. Are you deaf that you can't follow my orders? Or just stupid? What can I do with you?" continued the director of the asylum as if Ptah hadn't spoken. He moved away from the window to stand by a large, elaborate, wooden desk.

The walls of the large room were marble, as was the floor, and a long velvet rope hung in a corner of the room behind him that ascended to and through a hole in the ceiling. A heavily robed and hooded figure stood unmoving in the corner opposite the rope and behind the administrator saying nothing but observing all.

"You disrupt my work with the other patients, Ptah." The director sat slowly down on a rich, leather upholstered chair behind his desk. "You lie, cheat, steal, and bludgeon your fellow inmates. I am at the end of my rope."

"It's a lie," protested Ptah, wide-eyed, and disheveled, as two guards entered the room from a door behind him. "It's all lies!"

The guards grabbed him by each of his arm. He glanced at one, then the other, with a face distorted by fear. "Get your hands off of me! I have done nothing!"

"Yes, yes, are partially right, Ptah. It is you who is at the end of his rope."

The asylum guards jerked Ptah back off of his heels, unbalancing him.

"They had forgotten my medication!" objected Ptah, trying to yank his arms free of their grasp. "They wouldn't listen to me! I was just…'"

"Take Ptah to the tomb," the director interrupted, commanding the guards with the wave of his hand and in a tone they could not mistake.

"No!" Ptah screamed, struggling against the two men as they dragged him to and out the open door of the administrator's office. "No! I'm innocent! Stop! Stop! Have Mercy! Not the tomb! Oh, God. You can't do this!"

The heavily cowled figure behind the director moved gracefully to the window as the door closed behind Ptah and his two guards. The asylum's director tapped the window with his knuckles, startling the pigeons on the ledge that rose like a thrown scattering of wheat into the air.

"They are entering the building," said the person whose face was hidden beneath the hood. "Rajesh Dakkar and the men who follow him blindly. The tall man, the one with the little mustache and the crook, is…interesting. I believe he is French. The others are all distasteful. Do they all have to die?"

"Interesting," repeated the director without turning his head. "Interesting? You surprise and disappointment me. I would have thought you would have preferred Dakkar."

"I am also surprised. I thought you knew me better than that. Their leader thinks he's better than everyone. I don't' like men who think that."

"Ah. Forgive me; I forgot that. He is better, however. Unlike us, he may even be able to read the Atlantean document he intends to steal. Like Prometheus who stole fire from the Gods to benefit mankind, he intends to steal that document not for his benefit, but to help all of mankind. However, the Gods sent a monster to eat Prometheus' liver after they caught him."

"I intend to eat Dakkar's liver as well. Perhaps, with a little salt and pepper."

"Nevertheless, I expect more discernment from a Soter of your standing. Remember, death and I respect no man. Are you sure you don't want to keep him as a pet?"

The hooded person snorted and pushed the hood back on a beautiful, chestnut-brown face with large, blue, almond-shaped eyes, a comely nose, and full lips beneath a wealth of thick, black hair. The back of her right hand laying at the base of her neck was tattooed with the Soter open eye with an Ankh centered in its pupil. Her mood was somber.

"Not funny," she said, flatly. "My standing is as just one of your flunkies, no more and no less despite my birth, and I expect to receive no special treatment."

"Good. For future reference, you need to remember that no one, and I mean no one, talks to me in that tone of voice. And I assure you that you receive no special treatment. 'Once the game is over, the king and the pawn go back into the same box.'"

"No one, perhaps, but my father?" asked the woman rhetorically. "I am neither king nor pawn. Did you forget? My name is Soma."

His two guards shoved Ptah through the open doorway of a cell and threw him hard to its stone floor. Ptah struggled up from where he lay on his left forearm.

"Let's see you suck opium from stone, maggot," snarled a guard.

"Rot in peace," added the second guard. "You stinking, crazy, old fool."

Finished insulting their prisoner, they turned, chuckling, exited the cell, and jerked the door shut behind them.

As Ptah rose quickly from the floor, he heard an iron bolt fall into place on the other side of the door, and the sound of rapidly receding footfalls. Without hesitation and his face now completely drained of fear, he walked to the door. He began pounding on the rough, wooden planks of the cell door with his balled fists in a fury born of rage.

"Come back!" he screamed and struck the unforgiving door."You can't leave me here!" He struck the door again. "sob I'll s-stop. I swear it! Come... back..."

He pounded the door until his fists were bruised and his strength was exhausted, then he lay his open palms with his right cheek between them against its rough planks. In an instant, his expression of rage was replaced with a faint smile of cunning as if he were listening intently.

"Come...back..." he whispered.

After several moments of focused listening, and satisfied that his need was met, Ptah stepped away from the door and turned to face his cell. It was pitch black except for a grid of weak light thrown on the brick wall to his left through a barred window set high in the opposite wall. That light lit a grinning, human skeleton propped up against the wall, completely stripped of flesh and partially covered with a decaying robe. Silence lay like a blanket in the cell.

Motes swam in the shaft of light, and the air was dank, still, and stifling hot. He did nothing to disturb either as Ptah placed his left hand on the wall closest to him and pushed a hidden stud with certain knowledge. Deep in the bowels of the catacombs of the asylum, water rushed through a web of cooper tubes. Steam hissed through those tubes and screamed through substations until it reached and turned the hidden gears that slid stone against flagstone in the floor of his cell. From a snail's view, Ptah took several steps forward into the cell and sank into the floor up to his knees.

He took another step down into a now open and visible stairwell that had been seamlessly hidden in the floor only moments ago, and sank up to his waist. His third step left the cell above him empty and lifeless as the earlier grating sound of stone on stone once again violated the silence that then diminished and fell away. The opening to the stairwell had vanished.

At the bottom of a long fall of steps, Ptah stopped and looked back up at the trap door of faux stone that had shut tight above him, then turned and moved down a tunnel that had obviously been enlarged by human hands. The clammy tunnel was lit with what seemed to be haphazardly spaced torches embedded in the walls that threw dancing shadows everywhere.

As he walked, his hard-heeled leather sandals echoed with a sharp sound like nails driven into wood. Ptah ignored the sound and, from long familiarity, also paid no heed to the first of a series of rough, shallow niches that had been chiseled from the walls; the hooded, human skeleton slumped inside in rotten clothes smiled eternally at him with a mouth full of broken, decaying, yellow teeth.

The second was the twin of the first, but the third niche he passed exhibited a veined statue of an Englishman, his arms thrown up before his face in an utterly vain attempt to defend himself against something utterly monstrous and so horrendous that it had frozen his blood in his veins. The cracked and pitted statue looked like living flesh turned into stone.

"What a bloody pity," Ptah said to himself in mock concern. "At least he got no more and no less than every English twit deserves."

Ptah stopped at an entrance without a door not far from the foot of the stairs. Without hesitation, he said "To agree with Nechops is superfluous; to disagree is death. I bear a message from Orosius, the 'lamp merchant.'"

"Enter, Ptah," answered a powerful, bass voice from beyond the entrance.

"What brings my loyal employee here at this place and time? I hope good news for the brotherhood."

Ptah crossed the threshold without ceremony or hesitation. The torches embedded in the room's walls cast only a weak, flickering light on the man standing in its center on an otherwise empty chamber. Nevertheless, Ptah could see that, three yards behind him, there was a second entrance, this one with a hung and closed door.

Ptah could also see that the powerful mien of the man of only average height and build radiated absolute confidence and unquestionable authority. He wore the ceremonial, hooded robe of the High Custodian of the Soters, and an open eye with an Ankh pupil was painted on his forehead. His long, black hair fell to the hood pushed down around his neck.

"Is this timely?" Nechops asked quietly. "I am busy today. We prepare the tomb for a fallen brother. Our hearts are heavy."

"Who is so honored, Lord Nechops?"

"Another of our employees; Serapis, who failed to regain the map in Delhi, Ptah."

"Oh, dear. He is dead?"

"Not yet. What says Orosius, the lamp merchant, Ptah?" asked the High Priest. "Has he received a new shipment of genie filled lamps?"

"No. Orosius says Dakkar is in Alexandria."

"Ah. Your information is welcome and timely. Time is short. Follow me," said Nechops, as he grabbed Ptah's left arm with his right hand to guide him to and through the door behind him into a short tunnel ending with another closed door.

"It is an exciting day, is it not, Ptah?" said Nechops as they reached the door. "A whole gaggle of men will be able to answer the great question that has always puzzled man; of what waits for us after death."

Nechops opened the door and both of the Soters entered another small room that, created centuries ago from a bubble captured in lava, had been improved by their hands.

Before them, two hooded acolytes were testing the strength of hempen cords that bound the hands of a gagged man lying on the room's stone floor. They did not acknowledge Ptah or Nechops.

The prostrate man's dilated eyes, muffled groans and screams were the stuff of naked fear as he thrashed and struggled against the men who knelt by him next to an ancient oblong crypt of basalt.

Satisfied that the cords would hold, the two acolytes rose from the floor, moved to the crypt, and, grasping its lid, began to push it off of the coffin to the rasping of stone grinding against stone.

"You men, there!" barked Wayne Downing, the First Mate of the Nautilus. To grab the attention of several of the brigs sailors, he slapped his big, open palm on the port side railing where he stood on the brig. "Get that hold open. Now. The quicker we get this ship restocked, the faster you earn shore leave!" *And get drunk out of your lazy minds* he added in his head.

An enthusiastic yell and universal grins from the crewmen were the response he won as some of Dakkar's men continued to secure a small hoist to one side of the already open hold.

Downing was not a easy man to ignore. Built like a boulder, with a powerful jaw always peppered with whiskers, bushy eyebrows and a face like rock, the crew called him The Bear under their breaths when they weren't busy cursing him.

Almost below notice, the Nautilus rocked on the dirty, slate grey waters of the oldest port in the world, the west harbor of the ancient Port of Alexandria, Egypt. It lay on the West Verge of the Nile Delta between the Mediterranean Sea and Mariut Lake.

Downing spat a dirty brown stream of chewing tobacco over the side of the ship, then wiped his mouth with the back of a hand.

As familiar and unnoticed as the smells of home were to the first mate, the air in the polluted harbor hung heavy with the equally well-known, sour smell of human sweat, of fish, fertilizers, molasses, timber, grains and flour. His long experience on brigs and his frequent voyages to Egypt in the past were why he had been hired by Dakkar to command the Nautilus. Understandably, he had sighed when his captain and his captain's landlubbers, the Black Knights, had left the brig earlier. Landlubbers were always nothing but a nuisance and a pain in the butt, and these particular ones were little more than a cackle of clowns. Therefore, he was more than relieved when they had disembarked under the same sky of cerulean blue, and across the same gangway that would be used to restock the ship, and had quickly been absorbed in the ordered chaos of hardened men of every nation in heavy boots and rough clothing, and the smattering of equally rough prostitutes moiling on the docks.

"Good riddance," he muttered under his breath as Downing walked to the head of the gangway and eyed the dozen or so bored and impatient dock workers who lollygagged by two dozen or so containers at its foot.

They were obviously no strangers to this most active port in Egypt either, a port that had feed, clothed, and supplied Egypt with its needs since 1900 BC. Most of them looked like they would as soon as slit a man's throat, if the price were right, as manhandle heavy barrels of foodstuffs up the ship's ramp.

Downing pictured the two harbors that were separated by a T-shaped peninsula; the east port that was too shallow to be navigable by large vessels, and the west harbor where he had docked to restock supplies after the voyage from Palestine. He had been told by Dakkar that the captain intended to slip into Alexandra beneath the notice of the Soters, and that 'hiding' in the open was always the best course. That was only one of the ways that Downing knew that Dakkar was an idiot.

Satisfied with his survey of the motley dock workers below him, Downing waved his left arm like a windmill, and shouted down to them. They caught his shouted instruction, and reluctantly and none too quickly began to pick up the mostly wooden containers, predominately barrels of various sizes, and trudge up and across the gangway.

First Mate Downing removed a pencil from behind his big ear, and picked up a clipboard lying by the gangway as the first two men rolling a large barrel up that gangway reached him.

"What carry ye?" he demanded. The answer was slow in coming, so he barked, "Hurry up! I ain't got all day."

"Keep yer shirt on, mate. Potable water," said a well-muscled, black man, stripped to the waist but still wearing thick gloves to protect his hands as did the other workers.

"Watch yer mouth," Downing answered and directed them with a wave of his arm to the hold.

"What carry ye, ye filthy mug?" he asked of the second man to arrive carrying a smaller barrel hoisted up on his left shoulder.

"Salt meat," was the answer he received, and the same wave of his arm cleared the mouth of the gangway for the third dock worker. "Any chance it be grog?"

"Biscuit."

"Haul it aboard, and make it quick."

One by one, the barrels, trunks, or boxes were carried or rolled up the gangway and then to the hold where they were carefully handed to a relay of Dakkar's crew on the stairs and the floor of the hold, or where they lowered into storage by block and tackle. The single line of men trudging across the gangway became a double, parallel line as those who had already deposited their loads passed those boarding the ship until the last man carrying two, small, wooden kegs, one of each shoulder, reached Downing. Weary of the whole operation, he nevertheless eyed the worker with suspicion.

"Declare," said Downing to the bald-headed, fat man with a large earring in his left ear and a thick stub of a cigar in the left corner of his mouth. His long sleeved, muslin shirt was wet with sweat at his armpits, and he wore a dirty, checkered handkerchief tied together at its corners as a cap.

"What the hell is that?" asked Downing, pointing his pencil at the worker's mouth.

"This," asked the fat worker, talking round the cigar. "Finest a pauper can buy, matey. Egyptian. Want one?"

"Are yea an idiot. No fire on this ship. Toss it overboard."

"Not lit."

Anxious to join his mates at the nearest pub, Downing mulled his options over in his mind, and chose the way of least resistance.

"Keep it that way. What are ye carting on board me fine ship?"

"Salt of th' earth."

"Pass," grumbled Downing, already bored with the mundane duty of recording what Dakkar had pre-arranged to be loaded on the ship at its arrival. "But watch yourself."

"Much obliged," the worker said, and added *yer dirty bilge rat* in his mind as he tipped an imaginary hat, walked to the hold, and stopped at its lip. He looked down at the first sailor waiting for the next container midway up the stairs.

"I'm the last one, mate," he said. "Salt."

"Good and good. It's hot as hell down here, and I'm in need of a stout drink. Let's get this done. Hand it down, and be quick about it."

"Make it easy on yourself," said the dock worker, grinning. "You and the others are all finished with this. Go get a grog; I'll carry it down."

"Done and done!" said the sailor, waving the two other crew members up as he began to climb the stairs. "And thank much! Could you direct us to the nearest gin mill?"

"Sorry; I don't drink."

After the last sailor had left the hold and passed him, the bald man descended and carefully laid his keg on the floor close to the other barrels, ship's furniture, crates, hampers, bales, iron-bound boxes, and casks. He looked around the hold, and then up the stairs, and smiled.

He moved behind a stack of containers high enough to conceal his bulk and waited until the cover of the hold fell down and into its place. In the half-light, he left his hidden niche and returned to his small barrel of salt.

He knelt by the keg, pulled a tiny bung out of the side of one of the keg, then took out a long fuse from his pants pocket. He inserted the fuse in the keg.

He stood up and carefully carried the keg to a spot behind several other containers. He sat it down behind the boxes, and then surveyed the storage room again.

Satisfied that he was still alone, the fat man pursed his lips as if he were whistling and removed a small, cardboard box from his pants pocket. He opened it, and removed a phosphorous match.

"I be the way, the truth, and the light," he blasphemed, and struck the match on the rough side of its box and tossed the box away. He lit his cigar.

The fat man laughed without sound, then knelt by the keg again.

He lit the fuse with the cigar.

He rose from his knees, ran to the stairs, and ascended them. Holding his lit cigar close to his left thigh to hide it from Downing, he walked casually to the starboard railing of the Nautilus. He noticed that the first mate was checking his list and ignoring everything else.

The fat man stopped at the railing.

He yelled, "Fire in the hole!"

Downing looked up from his clipboard.

The fat man waved his lit cigar at Downing, and jumped overboard.

The Nautilus exploded.

The impact threw many of the dock workers on the pier off their feet.

First Mate Wayne Downing was shredded.

A fireball rose from the brig and grew into a mushroom cloud of shards wood, metal, canvas, biscuits, and human flesh.

The nearby prostitutes covered their heads to protect their hair from the rain of fire.

As the remaining ruin of the Nautilus burned in the harbor, the two acolytes below the main floor of the insane asylum slid the lid to the crypt to the floor and leaned it against the tomb.

"So says Nechops, Most Exalted High Custodian of the Library of Alexandria" said one of the hooded guards. "Through this doorway into Eternity comes Serapis; we write his name in blood in 'The Book of the Dead.'"

"Amen and amen," added the other Soter.

Then as Nechops and Ptah watched, they lifted their struggling prisoner from the floor and moved him over the open mouth of the crypt as, "Uuum!" their intended victim screamed into his gag.

His muffled shrieks did nothing to hide the writhing squishing squirming sound of some living horror coming from the open crypt.

Chapter Twelve

Rajesh's six Black Knights fidgeted with nervous anticipation and suspicion just within the threshold of the entrance to the foyer of the insane asylum. The yellow, plastered walls of the small, dingy room before them were skirted by a continuous wooden bench. On those stained benches sat an old man wearing a dead chicken tied on top of his head and what may have been his aged wife, a young woman applying greasy makeup on a face already caked clownish white with cosmetics, and a man curled up into a fetal ball. To their right and immediately in front of them were two closed doors that extrapolation suggested opened into the asylum. To their left, a rectangular opening had been cut in the wall opening onto a small adjacent room; a woman standing behind this opening studied each of the Knights in their turn as she talked to Dakkar standing before her.

"May I help you," the woman asked of the captain when she was done categorizing his team by their physical attributes. She liked the Frenchman.

"Yes," said Rajesh. "I need to speak to your administrator about placing a man suffering from violent and illogical outbursts in your institution."

"He's awfully busy today," said the woman. "I'm not certain that he can see you now."

Dakkar pulled a small, cloth bag from his left pocket and let it fall on the ledge at the bottom of the window in front of the woman. The bag rang with the muffled ching of coins.

"Which man," she asked as her eyes traveled from one Knight to the next with an expression of caution mixed with curiosity.

"The little one," said Dakkar, grinning.

"Hey!" Olaf yelled, surprised, and then added a long line of invectives and curses as he furiously hopped in place and threw his arms around like an ape.

Andrew tried and failed to subdue him. It was the greatest performance of Olaf's life.

"I thought so," said the receptionist.

The frantic man being lowered into the open mouth of the crypt screamed and screamed and screamed into his saliva soaked gag, and bit through his lower lip as, slowly, he sank into a wriggling soup of horror.

"The time is right," said Ptah to Nechops, "and my hand is quick. Let me kill him."

"Kill who?" asked Nechops, his arms crossed on his chest. "Certainly you cannot mean to kill my soon-to-be former employee, Serapis, about to 'nap' in the crypt? Are you suggesting you can do a better job with him than my servants, Ptah?"

"No, no, of course not, Nechops. I mean, let me kill Dakkar now."

"You are betrayed by ignorance, Ptah. Shall I remove it and your tongue?"

"Forgive this fool his impertinence," answered Ptah, lowering his head in submission. "So...what do we do with Dakkar and his men?"

"We, Ptah? Have you ever seen blood on my hands? Nothing, my local friend. We do nothing at all. The library is hungry. Let it feed. For is not the most tempting trap an open door?"

The lower half of the man's thrashing body had sunk into the white muck of wriggling, living horrors.

"Forgive my ignorance, my Lord. But where is Serapis' comrade?"

"Beneath Serapis."

"And what feeds in the tomb tonight?"

Only Serapis's face remained above the soup of swarming putrescence that filled and spilled over the lip of the crypt, moiling like a boiling pot of rice, writhing up and under the edges of his gag into his mouth, crawling over his upper lip into his nostrils, sucking at the outer edges of eyes dilated with terror, and leaving tiny trails of slime.

"Maggots," said Nechops.

"So the admission of a patient to my asylum," said the asylum's administrator, "was a ruse on your part, effendi. You are here for information leading to the location of the ancient and famous Library of Alexandria. You aren't the first, Mr.....?"

The administrator shuffled a stack of papers on his cluttered desk. Next to the paper stood an ink blotter and ink pot, and a quill pen in an ink pot. On the wall opposite the asylum's director was painted a grid of light

...he sank into a wriggling soup of horror.

thrown from a window opening onto the outside of the insane asylum. Emotionless, Rajesh Dakkar sat across the desk facing him. The long feather of the quill pen partially obscured his vision of the Greek.

"Dakkar," he answered, placing the thumb of his right hand on his cheek and cupping his remaining fingers on his chin. "My name is Rajesh Dakkar."

"You aren't the first to mistake legend for fact, Mr. Dakkar, but nothing remains of the city's magnificent library and museum. Not one brick. Not one scrap of paper," continued the administrator as Dakkar reached into the left, front pocket of his pants. "Surely as an archaeologist, you know they were razed by fire long after their contents had been gutted and destroyed. The Archbishop Theophilus burned them down centuries ago."

"I thought it was Arab invaders," said Dakkar as he dropped a small bag filled with coins on the administrator's desktop.

"Be that as it may, we are an institute for the treatment of the insane," said the administrator, leaning forward and stroking his chin as he stared at the bag of coins. He straightened in his chair, smiling. "Our job is to protect the innocent citizens of Alexandria from violent madmen."

"And recognition of your fine work," said Dakkar, "is certainly long past due."

"Yes. Yes, it is," said the director as he picked up the bag. "We have a storeroom filled with the flotsam of the mad. But I assure you that this debris doesn't include any forgotten treasures."

The administrator rose from his desk and moved to the corner of the room where the grid of light was disrupted by his body. He grasped the rope that dangled from an opening in the ceiling. Rajesh rose from his chair as the Arab pulled the rope.

An unseen bell chimed.

"One man's garbage," continued Rajesh as the door behind him opened and a man entered to stand in its threshold. "...is an archaeologist's treasure. If I find any...garbage...that interests me, might it be for sale?"

"Certainly. Certainly. We are always underfunded."

"Wonderful, sir. I am certain I will not leave empty handed."

"Take whatever you desire," said the director, and turned his back on the Nautilus' captain.

The man dressed in the traditional robe and keffiyeh headgear walked to where Rajesh stood and placed a hand on his back to guide him out of the room and through the door. He and Rajesh left the room.

"I have," mumbled the administrator as he opened the bag, took out a coin, and dropped the coin into his upturned palm.

The door that was opened did so onto an austere room of wooden walls, ceiling, and floor empty except for Rajesh's Knights and a second closed door in the opposite wall. Singh and Lagle startled in front of the door when it opened on their captain and his escort. To their right, both Chops knelt on the floor, throwing dice, and to their left, Andrew sat on the floor with his back to the wall next to the entrance. Olaf leaned with his back against that same wall. Andrew's crook lay next to his left leg.

"Arise, my Black Knights!" sneered the dwarf, pushing away from the wall as Rajesh stepped across the threshold. "We stand on the threshold of knowledge and power, by gar. Behold...the Prince of Atlantis!"

"Master!" exclaimed Singh with obvious relief. "We were growing worried," he added as he swabbed his bald pate from front to back with his right hand. He pressed his palms together in an attitude of prayer. "Finally."

"merodks," said Aiguo, snatching up his dice as his cheeks blushed a deep red.

"pridmak," added his twin, grinning sheepishly.

"Sirs," said Dakkar, "I have received the permission I sought. Please follow us."

As Rajesh followed his indifferent guard who was now in the middle of the room, Singh came alongside his captain and whispered, "Have you no fear this could be a trap? The Soters..."

"...hear your every word, old friend," Dakkar interrupted, his own voice lowered as well. "Be guarded in what you say," he added as Olaf and then Andrew joined them.

"Then why jeopardize lives, sahib?" Singh whispered as the administrator's assistant unlocked and then opened the second door and welcomed them all to enter with a wave of his hand. "There must be a better way."

"The quickest way to a jackal's lair," said Rajesh in the same subdued voice, "is to let the beast drag you there. Remember. We have no time to waste."

Rajesh, Indra, Olaf and Andrew stepped past the Arab into a tiny, dirty room, its wooden walls lined with shelves filled with small, mostly clay, jars, bowls, and vats, and an odd assortment of boxes of different sizes. Large wooden crates of various dimensions were also stacked against several of the shelves as well as in random columns on the floor.

"I think I've been a fool," said Olaf with his balled fists on his hips.

"O think you were born that way," added Henny as he entered the room behind his mates.

"Sirs," said Dakkar, standing in the middle of the room, "the adventure begins." As he spoke, their guide backed out of the door behind the Seven, closed, and locked it.

"If he thinks that lock will hold us," said Olaf, pulling his ear with his left hand, "he's got another think coming."

"Not now, Mr. Templeton," interjected Rajesh. "Instead, our first step must be to search these shelves for any container large enough to hide a thick document or scroll." He moved to a shelf and picked up and examined a large jar.

"Master," said Singh as he also moved to a shelf. "Why would they hide such a treasured document in so common a place, especially since they know you covet it?"

"It is at least distantly possible, Singh, that knowing my intent and reputation, they would anticipate that I would reject the first and most obvious guess outright and, therefore, hide the document in just such a place. Consequently, I can leave no 'stone' unturned."

With his own hand on a jar, Olaf said, "I have traveled some thousands of miles for this? This junk is the treasures of Atlantis?"

"Mr. Templeton," responded Rajesh with an expression on his face of growing petulance, "you speak before you think, which is regrettable since you often speak the nothing you thought."

Templeton picked up a pottery shard from the shelf and said, "I speak? By Gar, the vunderkind of India got mush for his brains. This is worthless crap."

Instantly, Rajesh seized Olaf's wrist with a vise-like grip.

"Enough" he said with ice lacing his voice. He released his grip, grabbed the dwarf under both armpits at the sides of his ribs, and jerked the struggling, humiliated, and furious Swede bodily off of the floor.

"My patience with your whining is completely exhausted. Hold your tongue or you are out of this expedition, now!"

Olaf snarked, "You can kiss my undulating…?"

Crack!

At the horrendous sound, Olaf glanced over his shoulder and down.

Rajesh threatened, "Sir, you presume too much. You are…?" and looked down in the same second. "…fired!"

The storage room floor split open down its center with the tortured sound of raw stone grating against raw stone, and its two halves began to sluggishly separate as they fell apart and open.

Dakkar dropped the dwarf and seized a bookshelf. Olaf fell to the floor, seizing his captain's left leg, and yelled, "Godt in Himmel!" as the pillars of crates in the room tottered and then collapsed, and a cacophony of jars and bowls and vases and boxes began to slide and fall out of their shelves.

"Sacre Bleu!" Andrew yelled, and, standing on the collapsing half of the floor opposite his captain and Olaf, turned at hearing the dwarf's words and instinctively leapt across the growing breach. He snapped the crook of his staff around a bookshelf to anchor himself as he turned to locate the dwarf. Seeing Olaf safely clinging to Rajesh's leg as a bucket and a small box of pottery shards rolled by him into the widening maw, Andrew looked back at Henny and the Chops on the collapsing floor where he had stood only a moment ago.

"Ach du Himmel! My boots are..." Henny yelled as he clung to the bookshelf with the Shepherd's Crook in a hail of falling crockery, his body almost vertical with the floor, and with Aiguo clutching his right boot that slowly inching its way down the Prussian's ankle. Bohai, perilously close to the gaping aperture, was clinging to Lamb's knees. A wooden crate slide down the floor, struck Pork a glancing blow, and disappeared into the maw.

"kmzptaq!" cried out Lamb.

"kmzptaq!" added Pork, as Andrew reached out and seized the China man's right ankle.

At the same instant, Singh cried out, "Master! Master!" as, thrashing about, he slid into the yawning mouth of the black aperture.

"Olaf," Rajesh yelled over the growing rumble of sliding and falling debris, "hold on!"

"Godtdammit!" cried Olaf, "I...I...can't..."

"No!" groaned Legrand. Horror laced his words. "It...?" He watched Olaf and Rajesh lose their anchoring grips and, frantically trying to find anything to grab to save themselves, begin to slide into the widening aperture.

"Olaf!" Rajesh yelled a final time.

"Aaaaa—" screamed Olaf as he slid into the black cavity in the floor. "Save Meee....."

Dead weights and with their limbs flailing, Olaf and Rajesh fell down and down and down in a shower of debris through utter darkness with the light of the room above them diminishing until first the dwarf and then Dakkar struck something below with bone-jarring impact.

And lay still in a chaos of debris, their eyes closed and their breaths broken and shallow.

Chapter Thirteen

Nemo looked up from where he sat at his massive desk as the Nautilus increasingly rocked back and forth from the volcanic tempest that churned the ocean above, then looked down at his quill pen and continued to write in his diary:

> Two hundred years before Christ, Hecataeus wrote he found himself in a square peristyle of the Library. Its sides were 120 yards long, it's ceiling a single block of dark-blue stone, glittering with stars.
>
> Columns twenty-five feet high supported this ceiling, each differently carved from a massive block of stone.
>
> Then Hecataeus stood before another doorway, decorated in relief and overlooked by three giant statues. The largest towered over its neighbors. This statue was of the Egyptian Pharaoh Ramses. Ramses' mother sat on the opposite side of the doorway with Ramses' daughter on her knee. On it's base was inscribed..."I am Ramses, King of Kings. Whoever wishes to know how great I am and where I am to be found, let him surpass one of my works."
>
> He and I were both fools.

Rajesh, laying prostrate on a flat, unforgiving floor and groaning, half opened his eyes. Olaf lay unmoving on the floor next to him, badly shaken and groaning as well. Above them, with the same grinding protest of stone against stone, the collapsed floor that was now the ceiling above them slowly rose and sealed itself closed.

Olaf rose on his forearms and looked over and beyond Rajesh's head. Dazed, confused and awed, he mumbled, "Jumping jiminy."

The captain of the Nautilus pushed himself up, first on his hands and knees, and then to his knees. He dusted off his pants with both hands as he followed the direction of Olaf's gaze, and smiled. Rajesh stood, and, offering a hand to the dwarf and helped Templeton rise to his feet as well. Around him, the remaining Black Knights were struggling to shake off the bruises and pain of their own falls as, one by one; they began to rise to their feet.

"It is as Hecataeus wrote, except the statues of Ramses and his mother and child have been changed," said Rajesh, his grey eyes riveted on the massive structure before him. "'I am Ramses, King of Kings; whoever wishes to know how great I am and where I am to be found, let him surpass one of my works.'"

"What...?" said the dwarf, his eyes huge. "Who was this Ramses?"

"What?" added Indra in awe as he helped Henny Lagle rise from his knees. The Prussian patted the leg of his pants that hid the dismantled rifle strapped beneath it.

"I've been in worst fixes, I guess," he said. "At least the musket is undamaged. Thanks for the hand up, brother Singh."

At the same time, Andrew rose to one knee and picked up his crook from where it lay on the stone floor. Aiguo, standing behind his twin sitting on the floor, repositioned Pork's backpack that had been twisted to one side by the China man's fall through the floor.

Then, one by one, the remaining Black Knights turned their attentions to the same monumental structure, illuminated by a multitude of burning torches bolted to the walls that had captured the undivided attention of Rajesh and Olaf. They all stared at an enormous stone statue, three times an average man's height, of the ancient Egyptian Pharaoh, Ramses, in the spectacular headgear of high station that stood rigid and flush on the left side of a massive door covered with vertical strips of hieroglyphics. To the right of the door, Ramses' mother sat with one arm resting on her left thigh and a child sitting on her right leg. The statues almost seemed to breathe in the eerie, dancing shadows cast by the cavern's multitude of torches.

"By gar, it's true! The Library?" said Olaf, pulling his ear with his left hand.

"No, Mr. Templeton. This is but the entrance to the Library of Alexandria," answered Rajesh. "But this does not concern us."

"Does not concern us, sahib?" asked Singh, unable to hide his consternation. "But, you said..."

Andrew cut Indra off. "The fall has addled his brain, M'sieu, oui?"

"Prince Dakkar? Is Andrew right?" Singh asked.

"A wise man," responded Rajesh, his eyes never leaving the door, "never enters the lion's den without marking an exit, Singh. First things first. Mr. Templeton, Andrew, Henny, Chop and Chop. It's time to build a pyramid."

As had been practiced to perfection dozens of times on board the Nautilus, Singh, Henny and Andrew, after handing his crook to Rajesh, moved close together to form the base of a human pyramid. Without hesitation, Aiguo and Bohai shimmied up their backs to stand on their shoulders. Lamb leaned down and offered his hand to Olaf who seized his wrist and was then hoisted up onto Andrew's and Henny's shoulders. A bit backward and overly careful, the dwarf then climbed up Aiguo back to stand on his shoulders.

Rajesh handed Andrew's Shepherd's Crook up to Singh. He passed it up by way of Bohai to Olaf who was only a yard or so short of the blue ceiling painted with white stars that, only minuets ago, had been the floor that had split apart beneath their feet.

"Look for any seam," said Rajesh, "or a device to trigger the opening of the roof again, Mr. Templeton. Please be careful."

"It's hopeless," said Olaf as he looked first to the ceiling and then down to respond to his captain, "in this light."

"Give it your best effort, Mr. Templeton," said Rajesh sternly. "If worse comes to worst, the quickest exit from the library would be the way we entered. So use the crook to very carefully search for any latch or device that we can use to again open that ceiling."

Olaf began to slowly swipe the hook of the Shepherd's Crook across the surface of the ceiling.

"What is that smell I smell?" said Andrew, wrinkling his nose.

"Phew. I smell it also, Andrew," Henny added. "It smells like Olaf's feet."

"Steady, men, steady," Rajesh warned as he watched the dwarf's progress. "You smell the fuel burned by the countless torches that must light the catacombs of his vast cavern. It is a smell that I cannot identify."

"I already did. It's Olaf's feet," said Henny.

"Anything, Olaf?" asked Rajesh.

"Nothing," said the dwarf as he still searched the ceiling with the crook of the staff. "No latch. No spring. I can't even find the seam again. These stars are painted with some glowing paint."

"Dismount, then, Mr. Templeton," called up Rajesh with a heavy sigh. "It is time to prepare."

With some effort, the human pyramid fell apart even more quickly than it had been assembled and five Black Knights stood awaiting Rajesh's next directions.

"I'm sorry," said Olaf as he returned the crook to Legrand. "I've failed you."

"You did your best, my little friend," said the Frenchman, and patted the dwarf on his shoulder.

"He's used to coming up a little short, yah?" quipped the Prussian.

"We have no time for that nonsense, sirs. Pay attention." Rajesh rolled up his black shirt from his waist to just below his ribcage to reveal the length of rope wrapped around his stomach. Aiguo and Bohai began to remove their backpacks as the remaining Black Knights also rolled up their shirts.

"Sirs, we must not be surprised again. At best, we are unwelcome guests of reluctant hosts."

"pezth," added Lamb.

"Fyrtsty," agreed Pork.

Their own black shirts raised, Andrew removed their coils of rope. Then the Prussian mercenary pulled apart a line of metal snaps running down his pants leg and removed the barrel of his musket.

"At worst," continued their captain with his uncoiled rope draped across his hands held in front of him, "we are thieves in the King's vaults. And the punishment is death."

"The broken floor was no accident, yah?" said Henny rhetorically. "You betcha. It was a trap."

Henny screwed the barrel to the stock of his rifle as two pieces of rope were snapped together by Andrew and Rajesh using the catches at the ends of each piece of line.

"And the torches embedded in these walls don't burn by themselves, Herr Henny. Further proof that we are not alone down here. Its important that we haven't been physically attacked, which helps to confirm my belief that only a handful of Soters maintain the library, and not as trained warriors."

Aiguo Chop snapped the tiny loop at the end of his reinforced rope to Rajesh's length as Bohai pulled a miner's helmet topped with a reflecting disk and candle from his opened backpack.

"There is no way back, my Black Knights, so we find another exit," the captain of the Nautilus said as he looked at the helmet in Pork's hands.

"Qoenoc??" asked Pork, his hunched shoulders expressing the need for direction from Rajesh.

"My feeling exactly, Pork Chop," said Henny. "Whatever you said."

"No, Chop. We don't need them just yet. But do save them. We certainly may have need of the helmets and their light for later. Sirs, prudence now directs us to the base of the statue of Ramses' mother, please."

In moments, the Seven Black Knights stood nervously, awaiting instructions, at the base of the statue that, seated, was nevertheless twice the height of a man. Andrew wore the coil of rope assembled from his crew members' individual sections coiled around his right shoulder.

"Was it to stop the Soters from killing us all?" said Henny studying the statue. "We won't exactly put the fear of God in their hearts with nothing but the rope, the gun, and the one sword."

"Oui," agreed Andrew. "It's almost enough to make oneself even wish Captain Dakkar's gas guns worked, non?"

"My sources say there are no more than eight priests," said Dakkar, ignoring Andrew's snide statement while studying the vertical strips of hieroglyphics on the massive door next to the statue. "Singh, join me please."

"Eight to seven," said Andrew, "its...good odds, my friend. But have you no fear this or another trap waits behind these doors?"

"No, M'sieu Andrew," said Rajesh. "Because we won't use those doors. Our ancient clue is that we must 'surpass' Ramses' work. That door," he said, pointing to the massive entrance, "opens on certain death for the uninformed."

"Singh...?" he added, waving a hand to direct his tutor to follow him, and moved to the door.

Rajesh and Indra studied the hieroglyphics carefully, Rajesh tracing some of them with the tips of his fingers, until they nodded in silent agreement at what they read. Then both men repeated their actions of moments earlier on an inscription on the left base of the statue of Ramses' mother. The captain of the Nautilus turned to face his expeditionary crew.

"Our next clue." concluded Rajesh calmly but as if he were still lost in his thoughts, "was in the inscriptions on the bases of both statues. To further answer your question, I have no fear, Andrew, because every step of this expedition was researched and planned well in advance. And because I am not without a surprise or two of my own."

"The collapsing floor was planned?" asked Andrew with an arched eyebrow.

Ignoring the Frenchman, Rajesh shoved his left hand into the front left pocket of his pants, removed his fist and opened it reveal five small, glass globes, looking much like transparent marbles. He smiled with hidden knowledge, then replaced the globes in his pants pocket.

"Ah, once again you are wrong, Olaf," grinned Henny. "He did not lose his marbles a long time ago. He got them in his pants!"

"M'sieu Andrew," continued Rajesh, "my tried and true man of action, it is time to lift a dwarf to your shoulders again, my friend. He needs to be elevated enough to raise our stony Queen mother's left arm at least six or seven inches up above her thigh."

"I was not a circus strong man! How can I lift…" Olaf began to object.

"Her arm, Mr. Templeton, rests on a hidden fulcrum. And with a large enough fulcrum, one can move the world. But you wouldn't know that; that isn't taught in the brothels and gambling dens where you learned to pick pockets and locks."

As Olaf gave his captain the "stink eye." Legrand knelt so that the dwarf could climb on his back, and then to his shoulders. Once the dwarf was there, the Frenchman rose slowly to his feet with some effort, bracing himself with his palms flat on the base of the statue.

"Push hard, Mr. Templeton," said Rajesh, pointing to the statue's giant forearm as he continued to watch Andrew. "Give it your best. Willingly entering one trap, M'sieu Andrew, to find the entrance doesn't mean I blindly enter another."

Olaf placed his hands around the giant stone forearm, and pushed it slowly up. Deep in the bowels of the library beneath the feet of the seven Black Knights, water churned in a gurgling boiler, violently boiled and hissed into steam. That steam screamed out of the boiler up and up through hidden, honeycombed webs of tubes in the stone walls of the cavern, through substations to their myriad final destinations, throwing unseen interconnected gears, lifting levers that opened or shut valves until it reached the statue's forearm and threw a switch that jerked an iron fulcrum into motion and a stone slab door slowly grumbled and slid sideways on a hidden niche in the floor.

"M'sieu? The collapsing floor. You knew," said Andrew, repeating his earlier question as he continued to balance the dwarf on his shoulders.

"I knew," said Dakkar as the hidden door in the statue's massive stone legs continued to grind open. "Yes, Andrew, as surely as the sun rises in the East, I knew.

"The map I purchased in Delhi not only showed me the location of the library in Alexandria," added Rajesh as Olaf jumped off of Andrew's shoulders. He waited to finish his thought as the Frenchman joined him, Singh, and the Chops to watch the widening maw of the hidden entrance. "It revealed the location of seventeen traps throughout the library guarding its priceless artifacts."

Singh shot a quick, challenging look at Rajesh. "Assuming the map isn't a trap as well, my Prince."

As Andrew and the Black Knights moved carefully into and then through the entrance between the Queen's gigantic legs, the Frenchman looked up and grinned.

"Deja vu," he chuckled.

"There is no need to be profane, sahib," said Singh.

"To be anything less would be to not be Andrew," grinned the Frenchman.

"Remember, sirs," continued Rajesh, ignoring Singh and the Frenchman, "no action we take will jeopardize the library's precious contents."

"Non? And what of our precious lives?" asked Andrew, and placed his right hand heavily on Rajesh's shoulder.

"I cannot hold one man's life above the..." Rajesh began, then jerked his shoulder from beneath Andrew's hand. "Please. Don't."

"Non?" asked the Frenchman with a faux expression of surprise that quickly deteriorated into disapproval. "Are you so very above me, my friend?"

"Don't be foolish. I believe all men are of equal value."

"You love things more than people, ja, Dakkar?!" asked Henny with naked sarcasm.

"peeg", Andrew added under his breath.

"Call me what you wish, M'sieu Andrew, I have ears like an owl, I am still the captain of this expedition. As for your statement, we have no time for debate, Herr Henny. We are here."

At a distance of six yards before the seven Black Knights stood three plain, closely spaced but equally large basalt doors. A stream of hieroglyphics on a marble plaque above them danced in the week light of two torches burning on the outer edged of both sides of the doors.

"This is somewhat odd," said Dakkar. "The walls of this peristyle should be painted with Ramses' war campaigns, but there are none. And two statues should skirt the three passageways that open onto the library. Therefore, there can only be one of two logical explanations. The first probable scenario is that the Soters knew that the Arab horde approaching Alexandria hundreds of years ago would certainly destroy the library. But they simply did not have the time necessary to exactly duplicate the architecture of the Library above in these caverns below..."

"Or two," interrupted Henny, "that this alternative entrance is also a trap."

"Agreed, Herr Lagle. Stay near," continued Rajesh. "Expect the un-expected, sirs."

"Maybe you tell that to Lamb Chop," said Olaf, pointing to the China man left of them at the edge of Rajesh's peripheral vision who was loping towards the middle of the three doors. Behind him, Pork furiously waved his arms, trying to stop his brother.

"My friend, M'sieu Chop! Stop!" yelled Andrew waving his crook.

"Stop him! Stop!" yelled Rajesh.

Abruptly, Aiguo "WRFBNSX!" screamed as paper camouflaged as flagstone shredded under his feet and the China man instantly vanished.

In the ceiling directly above, a stone slab slammed sideways in a wreath of steam and opened a second mouth above.

"Do they all have to die?" Soma asked. "All of them?"

She pushed her hood back and down to puddle around her neck as she watched the tiny image of Aiguo falling through the tear in the floor flutter within the great, crystal globe that rested in a niche atop a marble pedestal. A column of light falling from a large, square hole cut in the ceiling projected that image and the images of the Black Knights into the globe.

"Again?" questioned Nechops, shaking his head in disapproval.

"Again," answered his daughter.

That globe and pedestal stood in the middle of one of the innumerable, antediluvian bubbles varying from the size of a human fist to the size of Notre Dame that were created tens of thousands of years earlier by a horrific volcanic explosion, a violent, monolithic upheaval that had created the maze of caverns and tunnels that, long and weary centuries later, had become the subterranean library.

In addition to the globe, Nechops, and two chairs, the room contained a wooden table cluttered with folios, parchment, and scrolls, and a coal burning brazier adding light to the otherwise Spartan room. The hands of innumerable men had chiseled and beveled its walls smooth except for one recessed door and a cluster of rough-cut, square, stone blocks of differing sizes protruding from the wall behind Soma.

"Again," repeated Nechops with no emotion as he sat on the ancient, stone chair that had been placed before the crystal globe, studying the horrific scene before him. He touched the Eye of Horus with its Ankh pupil painted on his forehead from long years of thoughtless habit.

"I though we'd settled this long ago. You well know what our mandate was and is and shall always be: to gather all of the knowledge of the world into the Library, and maintain and protect it."

In the globe swam the soundless image of Bohai in extreme distress kneeling at the edge of the maw that had swallowed his twin. Andrew shifted from foot to foot at his side, unrolling their composite rope, and Henny watched Dakkar directing their actions with a sweep of his arm.

"From the destruction of the Library by the Arabs centuries past to this

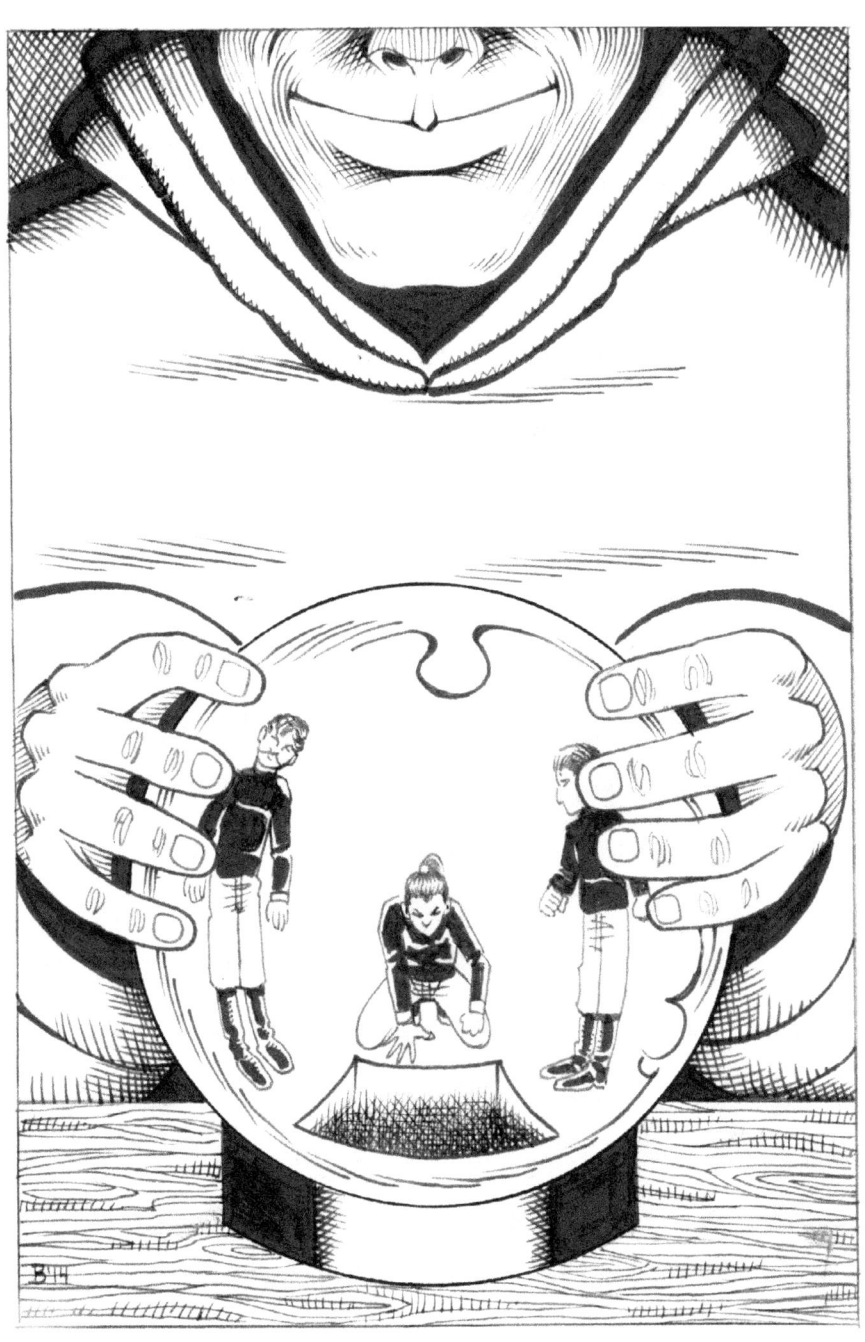

In the globe swam the…image of Bohai."

very day, grueling and painful experience has taught the Soters that the only way to protect the treasures of the Library is to deny them to anyone except the chosen. The Soters. To share them with anyone else only invites chaos and destruction."

"And how many dozens must die because, if the secrets of the Library *were* shared with the world, hundreds or thousand would die from the misuse of that knowledge, ignoring that great benefit and many lives might be saved as well? Who made you a god to decide who dies and who lives, father?

"I still believe," continued Soma, "that you have either misunderstood or even misapplied the mandate of the Pharaohs. I also believe that someday, somehow, someone will breach your death traps and not only reveal the location of the Library to the world, but its secrets as well. You cannot succeed in squelching the human thirst for knowledge forever. No one can. It's like trying to beat down the ocean's waves with a paddle."

"That's a very poetic and completely ignorant way of saying it, sweetheart," said Nechops. "I would expect no less from you. But my answer to your question about 'must all die' will be not only final, my beloved daughter, but more direct and to the point.

"Yes."

"eygssqkn" whispered Bohai, kneeling at the edge of the black mouth that had swallowed his twin brother. Having unrolled their composite rope, Andrew stood at Pork's side as Rajesh looked up at the second gaping mouth in the ceiling.

"Stand back, men, and don't move!" Rajesh commanded. "The hole in the floor was camouflaged with a sheet of paper painted to look like a flagstone, and there could be more! M'sieu Andrew! Get your rope down the hole! Herr Henny! I need a lamp, now, NOW!"

"There is the…" Andrew began, also looking up at the hole in the ceiling.

"NOW!" Rajesh shouted.

Anticipating his captain, Henny stood with one of the miner's helmet in his hands that he'd taken from Bohai's knapsack, its candle already lit with a phosphorescent match.

"Mr. Templeton!" ordered Rajesh, as Henny carefully knelt and directed the reflected light from the helmet down the maw. "Get over here! Hurry! You're going down. There still may be time…"

"Sacre Vache! I cannot see the bottom!" said the Frenchman.

Nechops stood up from his chair. He moved to the cluster of protruding, stone squares in the wall behind his daughter as Soma watched the image in the globe of the Frenchman's lips soundless mouthing words.

"Please," implored Soma in hushed tones. "Please. Not this time."

Nechops pushed the largest block of stone in until it was level with its wall.

Instantly, under intense pressure and with pile driver force, a column of scalding water exploded down with profane fury from the hole in the ceiling, striking the maw below and creating a blistering fountain that drenched the six Black Knights.

It exploded, knocking Pork and Henny like a balled volcanic fist back against a wall, tearing the musket from the Prussian's hand. The musket skimmed across the floor in circles until it struck a wall opposite Henny and lay still. As the gun struck the wall, the two barely conscious Black Knights slid down to sit on the floor.

An instant before it exploded, Andrew said, "Sacre bleu!" and was thrown back against a wall where he and his crook fell to the floor.

It exploded, and threw Singh like a broken doll back against a wall next to Andrew where he folded like a deflated accordion and slumped to the floor.

The Frenchman's hand slowly relaxed and fell open and the Shepherd's Crook slipped to the floor in a puddle of water beside him.

Pork irrationally leaned in towards the terrible, hurricane-force tower of super-heated death.

At the edge of the thundering pillar of scalding death and behind Bohai, Rajesh threw his right arm around the China man's shoulder and chest and grabbed his own left arm with his left hand in an iron grip to restrain Pork.

"OODCCKKKKK!" Pork screamed as he struggled against Rajesh to leap into the torrent.

"Chop! Chop! NO!" screamed Rajesh.

His words were swallowed by the roaring of the water as Pork struggled free.

"Chop! NO!" Dakkar screamed again as he threw up his right forearm to protect his face as Pork pulled free.

"CIDLSZUOPCKG!" screamed Bohai, but his guttural words were obliterated by the ear-splitting yowl of the torrent.

His face distorted with anguish and covered with tears, his hands roped into fists, and with his teeth clenched, the China man stopped just short of the blast of water and spoke not the Knight's slur of a nickname,

Lamb, but his brother's Chinese name, not for the sake of his ears, nor for the benefit of Rajesh behind him or the other Knights because no one could have heard it anyway, but as the final testament of his love for his twin to God.

Then he leapt into the geyser.

Rajesh stood frozen, his left hand stretched out in a futile gesture to somehow stop the China man's folly, his face distorted with disbelief, shame, and horror as a scalding spray thrown from Pork's body in the torrent drenched him.

For his sake alone, Rajesh said. "No.

"This can't have happened."

In his hidden chamber deep in the bowels of the library, Nechops watched as the rectangular block pushed itself out and stopped flush with the wall.

Drenched and groggy, Henny staggered up and pushed himself away from the wall that he had struck. On unsteady legs, he splashed his way through the half-foot of water on the floor to his musket and picked it up. Then he turned and moved cautiously to the left side of the screaming geyser, watching Singh move to its right side as he did so.

Rajesh said to no one, "It's not my fault."

The stone slab in the ceiling slid shut.

As if sliced by a knife, the column of water collapsed on the floor.

Rajesh stood at the lip of the abyss at his feet, now filled to its rim with boiling water that overflowed onto the floor, still steaming. His arms hung limp and his clothes clung to his body as the last vestiges of the geyser from the ceiling slowed to fat, noisy individual drops.

He whispered "Chop."

Despondent, Templeton, Singh, Henny, Andrew, and Rajesh, their clothing drenched and their hair matted, stood around the pool of steaming water that had eaten Bohai and Aiguo Chop for moments that seemed to stretch into eternity. Rajesh stood rigid and somewhat apart from them as if in shock.

He said, "The map....a lie."

Behind him and to his left side, Olaf tried in vain to squeeze the left sleeve of his shirt dry as he snarled, "I am a boiled lobster."

Chapter Fourteen

"**I**t's like shooting fish in a barrel," said Nechops.

Across from her father, Soma jerked upright from the tiny, flickering image in the crystal globe of the five drenched Black Knights standing at the edge of the mouth of scalding water that had drowned the twins. Her face a mask of restrained rage, she jerked the hood pooled at her shoulders up and over her long, black hair to hide the fury in her chestnut-brown face.

She said, "Coward."

She stomped to the room's single door, opened it, stepped through, and slammed it behind her.

Nechops moved to and then stood silently in front of the crystal globe and watched his daughter's back as the door slammed shut.

He said, "My flesh and blood," shook his head in disappointment, and began to pace back in forth in front of the globe, his hands interlocked behind his back, muttering. As he did so, his face began to flush a deep red, and he leaned into each step as his stride lengthened and carried him further and further from the crystal ball.

As he passed the room's table, Nechops reached out with his forearm and swept its priceless, ancient folios, parchments, and scrolls off to fall in a chaotic flurry of paper to the floor.

He said, "Damn!" and stopped to look at the snow of ancient manuscripts around the table. "Damn, and damn again! She's my *daughter*! My *daughter!*" he uttered, and then his own pent-up frustration became a fury that exploded.

Grunting, he grabbed the edge of the table and toppled it over on top of the chaos of documents already littering the flagstones.

Growling, he picked up the table's chair and, raising it above his head, threw it at the brazier of burning coals, knocking it to the flagstone floor. As it rolled back and forth in diminishing arcs, the glowing, red-hot coals spilled out and rolled in a hail of fire towards the globe.

He snapped, "NO!" and, startled, jumped after the coals, furiously cursing and kicking each fiery piece away from the base of the globe.

Then he stood immobile, his chest heaving, his passion spent, and stared at the shambles he had made of the libraries observation room. The Most Exalted High Custodian of the Library of Alexandria moved to the one chair still upright that stood in front of the globe and sat down.

Nechops buried his face and his three eyes in his hands and sobbed.

Olaf, Singh, Henny, Legrand, and Rajesh, their spirits sagging, their clothing drenched, and their hair matted, stood around the steaming pool shaking water from their heads, wiping it from their faces, or shifting their weight from one foot to the other for long, quiet, emotionally charged moments. With his right arm outstretched to touch his captain, Singh walked to Dakkar who still stood rigid and apart as if frozen.

As he did so, Andrew said, "This is a disaster. Where are the bodies?" not expecting an answer. "There are no bodies!?!"

"Ja, Andrew. They are kaput," added Henny in a voice outraged, exhausted, and disillusioned.

"Amazing feat of engineering," said Rajesh in an oddly hollow voice, cupping his fingers on his chin. "They've re-channeled a natural geyser to create this trap."

"Sahib? Are you hurt?" asked Indra as he laid a hand on his captain's shoulder. "Rajesh?"

Dakkar knelt at the lip of the aperture where the hot water was rapidly draining down the hole, and dipped his fingers gingerly into the remaining pool. Henny Lagle squatted by Rajesh's side.

"They are caught, entangled below," said the Prussian. "Or sucked through the outlet."

Olaf joined Rajesh, his balled fists on his hips, and his drenched red beret impossibly still firmly atop his head. The dwarf's red eyes squinted as he bit his lower lip.

"By redirecting and artificially damning it," continued Rajesh as if he were deaf to the words of his exploratory team, "the Soters also eliminated a threat to the library. It probably originates as an ancient, underground river."

"What noise is this?" demanded Olaf, his face as red as his eyes as anger replaced mourning. "Two men just died here, Dakkar! And you talk about 'amazing feats of engineering.'"

"Here is your smell, M'sieu Andrew," Rajesh continued, ignoring Olaf. He removed his fingers from the water and looked at Henny as if he were looking at an alien in another universe in another dimension in another time. He raised his right hand to his lips and tasted the substance on his fingertips. "Petroleum is evident in the water."

"What! What did you just say!? Ach du Himmel. Once..." the Prussian began, his own face marked with a growing anger. "Just once...!"

"Save your concern," interrupted the dwarf, "for a man, Henny. This is one cold blooded pig!"

"I am a scientist, sirs."

Overcome with emotion, Andrew bent down behind his captain, his right hand outstretched to snatch the Prince up by his neck.

"You...are...the...bastard, Dakkar!" he growled as Rajesh spun about to face him, a spark of understanding coloring his detached demeanor.

"Objective observation is a scientific imper—"

Andrew grabbed Rajesh hard by his white collar.

Andrew's flushed face brushed his captain's as Dakkar struggled back from the Frenchman's grip, his eyes averted from the Frenchman's blazing eyes.

"M'sieu, they were men and worth more than all the scientific methods of Earth!" snarled Andrew, shaking Rajesh by his collar.

"They are dead, M'sieu Andrew," responded Rajesh. "You bring them back."

The Frenchman exploded with irrational rage, snatching up Rajesh with his hands under his captain's armpits to hold him level with Andrew's face.

"As God is my witness, Dakkar," he growled, "I will break your neck!"

"Andrew," Singh yelled as he lunged toward the two men, "Put him down! Now!"

"Considering the circumstances, M'sieu Legrand," said Rajesh calmly, "I forgive your emotional outbreak."

Behind him, Singh grabbed the Frenchman by both of his shoulders as he snapped, "Andrew! What can you gain by this? You can't bring Lamb and Pork back to life!"

"I gain justice," Andrew answered, turning his head slightly over his shoulder to see who restrained him. As he did so, he partly lowered Rajesh as the initial heat of his rage began to drain away. "He gives not a damn for any of our lives."

"The need of the world," said Rajesh, calmly, "outweighs even my life, Andrew."

"Andrew...sahib...?" begged Singh as he swabbed his bald pate from front to back with his right hand. "You know this won't accomplish anything. Put him down. Gently."

Reluctantly, Andrew slowly lowered his captain to the floor as he averted his own face from Rajesh and Singh to hide his shame.

"I understand your frustration, M'sieu Andrew. But their deaths were not in vain," continued Rajesh as if nothing untoward had happened. "Because of this tragedy, I now no longer wholly trust my information," he added as he took a step back from the Frenchman.

Singh shook his head in disappointment and disbelief and sighed. "In some things, Andrew," he said quietly, "he is still a child."

As Rajesh began to walk away from the two men, the Frenchman said, "I'm begin to regret zee day he sent you as his agent to save my worthless skin, Singh."

"I understand your compassion for Pork and Lamb, and your anger, Andrew, but surely you must admit that Rajesh is not responsible for their deaths. Whatever his motive, it was Lamb who disobeyed the captain's direct order, and is therefore responsible for his own rash decision and death. And even I cannot fathom why Bohai jumped into the torrent. Was it a vain attempt to save his twin? Was it suicide driven by the tragic death of his brother?"

"All I know is that Dakkar is a lousy weasel," sneered the Frenchman.

"Not one of us can change what just happened," said Rajesh, now completely in touch with the present as he approached the three doors before him. "But we can mold our own lives, sirs, our own futures. I must admit I was wrong, and for that, I am sorry. But look down at your feet at the water left by the geyser."

He patted at the absorbed water and his initial guilt from his shoulder as he splashed his way closer to the three doors. "Now, logic and observation must guide us. The water on the floor is running down into the left door. Despite the map, that door must lead to the museum.

"Ah," he continued. "I was right. Water pools at the right entrance. We are about twelve feet below the streets of Alexandria. Therefore, this door is false as well."

As Rajesh stopped in front of the left of the three doors, Olaf joined Andrew.

"If his deduction is as accurate as his map," whispered Andrew to the dwarf, "we'll never find the door out, non?"

"Fear not my frog eating friend," Olaf smirked, putting his left hand into the left front pocket of his pants. He pulled out his fist, then opened it for the Frenchman.

Rajesh's five, small, glass globes rested in his open palm.

"It don't even matter if he is wrong again. We can make our own door."

Legrand glanced around to see if anyone else was looking at them, and then winked his left eye. "I think I love you, Olaf, you sly pickpocket."

"I'm surprised by you, my friend. I am no pickpocket, Andrew. I'm just a simple locksmith. And don't get all sentimental on me, you old fake. Go get your crook."

One by one, the sullen Black Knights joined Rajesh to stand before the door he now gingerly touched. "Good, he said, "good. It is not hot to my touch. I tested the door for heat because the Soters may have adapted other natural characteristics of these caverns as snares, sirs. M'sieu Andrew. Continue to test for traps with your crook."

"M'sieu Dakkar, test for them yourself," said Legrand and disdainfully thrust the Shepherd's Crook in front of his captain.

"Maybe, just maybe, you'll grow up, M'sieu," said Rajesh, perturbed, as he accepted Andrew's crook and began to tap with it on the doorjamb and then the surface of the door.

"My Prince," Singh objected, "let me do this. I am expendable."

"I am not a child, Singh, and you are every bit as valuable as any other Knight. When we are inside, men, touch nothing."

Rajesh carefully pushed the heavy basalt door open with the end of the crook and looked inside as his team gathered behind him. Seeing nothing that triggered fear or even caution, he entered. Singh, Henny, Olaf and Andrew followed as the Swede commanded silence from the Frenchman by touching his right digit to his lips. Andrew offered a knowing wink of understanding and a nod of his head.

"The petroleum and boiling geyser troubles me, Singh," said Rajesh to his mentor. "Did the Soters know of these potential threats to the library before they enlarged these caverns? I don't really think so."

As Rajesh spoke, Olaf paused at the rear of the team, placing his right hand on the doorjamb of the closed, middle door as he watched the receding backs of the remainder of the team.

"No," Rajesh continued. "They surely would have chosen another location to house the library's priceless treasures safely. The Soters must have known nothing about geology...or petroleum, hundreds of years ago."

As the Indian prince entered, Olaf placed his open right palm on the surface of the middle door as he watched the entrance to his left to see if his absence had been noticed.

"Then," Rajesh continued as his three team members proceeded, "if discovering these natural dangers as they dug, and deciding to safely re-channel each, what possible mishaps..."

"...lie ahead," Rajesh said as he and his men stopped just inside the open door.

"Zut!"exclaimed an awed Andrew. "We have found the lost mine of Solomon!"

Alone of all the caverns and passageways through which they had come, no vestige of raw, volcanic stone remained in the room in front of

Rajesh and the Black Knights. It was rich and splendid in its simplicity. Its floor and ceiling were meticulously tiled with green veined marble. A green and blue mosaic of two cavorting dolphins was inset in the center of the floor. The walls were pristine and plastered white, and two of them were hidden from floor to ceiling by mahogany book shelves full of bound folios, loose manuscript pages, and scrolls of various sizes. The remaining walls were painted with large aquamarine murals of one dolphin leaping over another dolphin on its back. Near the bookshelves to their left stood a golden podium supported on a thick column adorned with large seahorses. On the podium rested a huge, thick, open book.

Taller than the Frenchman, a marble statue of Poseidon with his trident balanced in his left hand stood in an opposite corner, dominating the room as it guarded its priceless contents. Poseidon's right balled fist rested on his hip. Also to the left side of the four men, a brass coal-burning brazier supported by a column of merfolk carrying it on their backs added additional light to that given by torches on the walls.

"Sirs," said Rajesh, "we stand in the presence of all that remains above the ocean of the great island of Atlantis." He presented the room to his men with the broad sweep of his right arm.

"Here are the secrets of an age long past, of the first stirrings of architecture, mathematics, philosophy, the arts, science, and much more. Here is the knowledge discovered by the world's first and best scientists who carried these folios, scrolls and manuscripts with them as they fled in magnificent sailing ships from their slowly sinking island-state to the coasts of Africa, Italy, Greece, Turkey, South America, and, yes, even America."

"Listen to me carefully, my Black Knights. Look for anything bearing an Atlantean cuneiform like two vertical, parallel bars with a crossing line that looks like its broken, or an 'E' with its open end closed by an additional vertical line."

Rajesh moved to one of the shelves on the stone walls and removed a volume as Andrew examined the stature of Poseidon and Indra and Henny approached the open book on its podium.

"We have stepped 10,000 years into the past, sirs," said the prince, replacing the volume. "These pieces may be fragile. Please, please, handle them as you would a priceless work of art."

"Sacre vache! It is beyond belief." said Andrew, touching Poseidon's hip. "This statue is magnifeek, non? Almost good enough to be by a Frenchman."

"Could this be the manuscript we seek, Dakkar?" asked Singh as he began to closely examine the huge book on the podium without touching it. "Why else would it be so displayed?"

"Or just a red herring," stated Henny without the inflection of a question as he also looked at the book at arm's length. "Remember the terrible fate of the Chops, Lamb and Pork, Mr. Singh."

Rajesh closed and returned the second book he had removed from its shelf. He removed a third bound manuscript to the left of three rolled scrolls.

"Be careful, sirs," he said as he gently turned one of its pages. "Experience has already taught the obvious can mean death. Remember my instructions. Does it bear an Atlantean cuneiform? The parallel bars or the closed 'E.'"

"Not even the a, e, i, o, or u, Rajesh," Henny mocked. "The writing is too small to read from here, mien Herr."

Rajesh closed the third dusty volume, replaced it, and began searching another shelf. The captain of the Nautilus picked up a manuscript lying there covered with dust, and wiped it clean. Under the skein of dust were cuneiform letters. His jaw slackened, his eyes widened, and his hand trembled as, in stunned awe, he whispered,"My God."

Not hearing Rajesh's words, Henny and Singh were leaning closer to the book on the golden podium, squinting as they tried to read a page. Rajesh glanced quickly around the room to see if anyone was watching him, then rolled the ancient manuscript into the shape of a u and carefully slid it under the left sleeve of his black shirt around his forearm.

At that moment, Singh said, "The best hiding place.." He pointed at a line in the book on the podium. "...is out in the open."

"This looks like the scrawling of a madman," added Henny, leaning very close to the volume. "Or of Olaf."

"Ha ha ha ha ha ha!"

The sudden, jarring, disembodied laughter broke the focus of Rajesh and his Black Knights, each instantly refocusing their attention on finding its source.

Leering Nechops stood in front of the doorway in the wall opposite the entrance to the Atlantis room. His hands were clasped behind him. His hood was pushed back and down to pool around his shoulders. Even the painted third eye in his wrinkled forehead seemed to sparkle with disdain.

"Welcome, you filthy little thieves!" he grinned. "I am Nechops, Most Exalted High Custodian of the Library of Alexandria. You may call me 'the last face I'll ever see.'"

"Zut alors??!?" interjected Andrew. "What the..?"

"It's another blowhard," added Olaf. "The spitting image of the captain."

"I know you've been dying to meet me," Nechops continued. "Please ...let me help!"

A stone slab fell down with the sound of muffled thunder behind Nechops, sealing the doorway.

All of a sudden, Nechops' eerily disembodied voice snapped, "Behind you, fools!"

The four adventurers turned on their heels. Defiant and cocksure, Nechops now stood in the entrance to the Atlantean room, his arms relaxed at his sides, his mouth a sneer, and his laughter replaced with sarcasm.

"But why," continued the Soter, "should I be surprised by the level of stupidity that has already cost you two of your 'Black Knights' by the simplest and most obvious of traps, Dakkar?"

Still behind his captain, Henny stepped closer to Rajesh and raised his musket to the level of his chest as Andrew readied his staff to club Nechops.

"Black Knights. I laugh in your faces. Your arrogance is incredible. You weren't 'expected'. You were lured here, as have been others, 'Prince' Dakkar! While thousands write, debate and wonder about the library..."

"Your threats, "Dakkar said, cutting off the Soter, "fall on deaf ears, Nechops."

"...only a handful are stupid enough to actually search for it," continued the Soter, deaf to Rajesh's interruption.

Rajesh lunged forward and thrust out his open right hand to touch Nechops only for his fingertips to jamb up against cold glass.

"He neither hears or sees us, sirs," said Rajesh without turning to face his crew. "This is a mirror reflecting Nechops' image from a distant and safe location. Coated glass on which Nechops has projected his person from a room or crevice behind him."

Seemingly ignoring Rajesh, Nechops continued, "Our most effective protection is to eliminate the handful."

"He cannot even hear us." Rajesh took a step back from the mirror, pointing at the image there. "Since we cannot go back the way we've come, we go through!"

"M'sieu Andrew! Strike!"

Andrew drew back his Shepherd's Crook, defensively closing his eyes.

"We enjoy the iron..."

Andrew struck!

Nechops' words were shattered as Andrew struck, smashing the glass, instantly creating a shower of deadly shards as Rajesh, Henny, and Singh shielded their faces with raised arms. In the same instance, a deadly cloud of gas began to hiss from some hidden vent behind the shards of shattered glass still clinging to the frame of the mirror!

"Through the opening!" Rajesh yelled, then slapped his right hand over his nose. "Watch out for the glass shards around the mouth!

"Now!" he yelled again and stepped onto the threshold.

"Sahib," Singh yelled over the hiss of the foul gas, "what of the manuscript!?"

"There's no time!" Rajesh barked over his shoulder. "They're releasing gas! It brings quick and certain death!"

Ignoring the furious scream of the cloud of gas, the Prussian turned away from Singh, Rajesh, and Andrew. One broad step brought him to the edge of the podium.

He stretched out his left arm to seize the book.

"Not without this," he gasped, and raised his hands to grab the outermost edges of the volume.

Rajesh stepped back from the hole in the shattered mirror, and with his free hand on the small of his tutor's back, pushed Singh partially through the ragged maw.

He visually surveyed the room.

"Where's Olaf?" he asked, as he searched the chamber for the dwarf.

"Where's Olaf?!" he repeated, knowing but denying the evidence of his own eyes.

"Where's Olaf?!" the Prince of Bundelkund yelled.

Singh turned in the threshold.

His and Rajesh's faces distorted with horror as they saw Henny seize the edges of the book.

"Henny! NO!" Rajesh screamed. "Don't touch it!"

Zap!

His hands on the book, his face twisted by surprise and excruciating pain, Henny shook and squirmed and jerked as his mane of blond hair rose in a shimmering halo and began to smolder and the stench of his burning flesh overpowered the smell of rancid gas.

Chapter Fifteen

As the volcano erupted, shaking apart the island and whipping the air into a frenzy above the blanket of ocean churning fifty feet above the Nautilus and its inventor, Nemo's hand and pen rose from his diary, momentarily hung, then fell to the page to write again.

I do not understand men. It is madness. They work against their own best interests and embrace what destroys them instead. Such was Olaf Templeton.

Alone, he could not break out of the squalor and degradation of poverty.

He was a freak and pickpocket for the Circus Maximus in Europe. The circus profited most when Olaf's hands were not in his own pockets.

I alone helped Olaf.

I had special need of men with unusual talents. Strength. Agility. A sharp eye and quick hands. Templeton had quick hands, an all-consuming greed, and no conscience. Olaf was an enigma. He had nothing. Nothing was ever enough.

He was indentured to risk a life he felt was worthless, and one he could not escape. He never offered gratitude. I would have paid him a king's ransom in gold. He wanted to be king instead.

The dwarf disappeared from the expedition at the threshold of the Atlantean archive. I never saw him again.

Did he save himself beneath Alexandria? Or do his bones rot in some murky crevice, forgotten and unmourned? No one knows.

No one cares.

I like to think he escaped. I like to suspect he pilfers the pockets and purses of the unsuspecting people of England or Turkey or Greece.

Whatever his fate, I know he could not escape one trap.

Himself.

As Henny Lagle silently screamed and burned and smoked, Olaf Templeton whispered, "pigs."

Olaf sat and laughed atop a fabulous mound of gold coins deeper than he was tall.

Through the open door behind him stretched a long hall with six doors on both sides of its walls ending at the closed, middle door that had been rejected as false by Rajesh. Olaf had anxiously tested, picked the lock, opened, and then abandoned the empty rooms behind each of those locked doors with growing frustration and the speed and ease of a well seasoned pick lock, driven by self-loathing, hated and all-consuming greed.

Speechless in his reverie, the dwarf sat and giggled and wiggled into the accumulated wealth of centuries in the otherwise empty, non-nondescript room, scooping up noisy handfuls of coins from the pile and letting them run like water through his fingers only to let them fall back on the mound with their own metallic laughter.

As he sat and showered himself with gold, the dwarf ruminated on the spit and punches and kicks, and heard again the hurled slurs of "freak" and "hump" and "toad" and worse that had tortured him all of his life. He relived the gnawing hunger and humiliation of poverty, the haughty looks of girls and women who made no attempt to hide their revulsion, of beatings by police and the stink of prisons, and the countless black nights filled with thoughts of homicide, genocide, and suicide.

He whispered, "pigs," a second time.

Then Olaf rose from the pile of coins to his knees, and, reaching behind and over his shoulders, seized his shirt, no, Dakkar's stupid black shirt, and pulled it up over his head, and then off of his body.

He stripped off his tools for picking locks from around his stomach and tossed the strap away.

He said, "We are rich men, Andrew!"

Olaf tied the opening at the wrists of two sleeves and the opening for his neck closed. His smile wilted and his eyes narrowed to slits as the blackest wound of his soul opened.

He said, "No. I am a rich man, Andrew. Just Olaf."

Then the Swedish dwarf filled his makeshift bag with as many of the gold coins as he thought he could carry, occasionally lifting his makeshift bag to gauge its weight.

"I think it will finally blow my way," he snickered.

His shirt bulging with treasure, Olaf gingerly stepped off of the pile of gold coins, scattering some like thrown seeds across the marble floor. The dwarf walked to the door of the room, being careful not to loose his footing on loose coins and dragging his heavy, makeshift bag behind him. Olaf began to sing a tune under his breath as he stepped out of the room into the long hall. He sang:

"London Bridge is falling down,
Falling down, falling down.
London Bridge is falling down,
My fair lady."
With the cocky self-assurance of a well-heeled thief, Olaf began to
stride down the hall as he continued to sing, carrying his bag in his right
hand.
"London Bridge is broken down,
Broken down, broken down.
London Bridge is broken down,
My fair lady."

Deep in an alternative observation room in the library, Nechops
pushed a rectangular block of stone into a wall.

To his right and behind the dwarf, three stone slabs fell with a heavy
thud, sealing three of the doors in the hallway shut.

Shocked by the sound, Olaf stopped and turned to stare for the briefest
of seconds at the sealed doors as three more stone slabs fell, sealing doors
in front of him.

His face distorted with a rapidly growing fear, Olaf's song fell apart as
he began to trot down the hall, slowed, however, by the awkward weight of
his bag full of loose coins.

Nechops pushed a second block into the wall of his hidden chamber.

A slab of stone in the ceiling behind the dwarf sprung open and Olaf
heard something huge strike the floor, hissing, and the sudden rushing
sound of fire in the otherwise silent corridor.

He glanced behind him, and fear soured into terror.

Olaf gasped, "Jumping jiminy!" to the only living thing who could hear
him, the Angel of Death that had surely shoved the immense ball of raging
white-hot fire that filled every inch of space behind him and down the hall.

Three more stone slabs fell, sealing most of the possible avenues of
escape for the dwarf.

Olaf dropped his shirt full of coins.

He began to run for his life as the huge, blazing fireball hurtled down
the hallway and after the tiny Swede.

The dwarf turned, threw his arms over his face, and stood, paralyzed
with terror, in the path of the huge, red hot fireball.

It rolled over and ate him.

...stone slabs fell, sealing doors in front of him.

As it ate Olaf, there was a quick, startling series of five explosions as Rajesh's secret globes that the dwarf had stolen exploded in Olaf's pants pocket.

Nechops pushed a third block into the wall of his hidden room.

A stone slab in the floor of the hallway slid open in front of the door that Rajesh had guessed false. The fireball struck the door, rebounded, and fell through the huge hole in the floor.

The stone slab slid closed.

Olaf's body lay on the hall floor, charred beyond recognition, half of his flesh burned from his skeleton, his limbs blown partially free of his torso. A scattered pile of gold coins radiated out from the burnt remains of his ruptured shirt behind his corpse.

His red beret lay close to his skull, still burning.

Nechops looked at the rectangular blocks of stone that had rebounded flush with the wall.

He said, "And that leaves four who would steal the sacred treasures of the library."

He turned and looked at Ptah standing behind him. Ptah's hands were on the back of a chair. That chair sat in front of a pedestal mounted with a large, slightly tilted mirror sitting in a dim funnel of light falling from an aperture in the ceiling above the two men.

"We owe a great debt," said Ptah, pulling the chair back slightly from the pedestal, "to all those who went before us who put such time, treasure, and sweat into these marvelous traps that protect the library, Nechops. The boiler that generates the steam that moves stone, the incredible system of mirrors that allows us to monitor those who invade the Library, and so much more. To use them wisely and well seems the best way to repay them."

"Indeed," said Nechops and sat down in the chair presented by Ptah who then pushed it closer to the pedestal. On the mirror, faint and slightly distorted, Olaf's corpse smoldered on the floor of the hallway where he had been slaughtered. Nechops grinned and placed the tips of his fingers together and held them level with his chin, his elbows on the armrests of the chair.

"And seven are now four," he summarized again. "At least briefly. Everything progresses as planned, as has been true so many times before, eh, Ptah? And, once again, what a man wants most shall kill him."

"Nevertheless, it is tragic, my Lord, that three Soter brothers died to protect the library for such as these. They were good men and true to the cause."

"Ptah, Ptah, Ptah." said Nechops, shaking his head in disagreement. "Would you have had Serapis and his comrade murder Dakkar on the streets of Delhi? What of the risk of exposing ourselves and the library if they'd been caught? All thing must be considered as we protect the holy treasures of eons past, no?

"Serapis and his men lured Dakkar onto the sea with our phony map. The failure of our 'werewolf' was regrettable but not unanticipated.

"Turn the mirror, Ptah. Another piece of our protective puzzle is about to fall into place."

Ptah winched at his master's disapproval.

"I understand the sacrifice, Nechops" he said as he did so, "but still mourn the loss. One of those men had been a close friend of mine since my early childhood."

Obediently, Ptah screwed the base of the pedestal around to his right to adjusted the mirror and reflect light from a different, overhead source. The image of Olaf Templeton's smoking corpse on the hall floor was now replaced on the mirror with Henny Lagle about to seize the edges of the great book on the golden pedestal in the center of the Atlantis room.

Nechops clapped his hands together like a child in anticipation of candy.

"Then you are a lesser man than Dakkar," Nechops continued, studying the image and smiling. "He understands that the loss of a few for the benefit of the many is necessary. Look! Look! More fun!"

Nechops paused to place his thumbs against his lower lip and his interlaced fingers at either side of his nose. "Some, as is this one about to seize the book, are 'fewer' than others."

"Ah. And unless Dakkar finds our hidden mirror in the room, we shall watch the results of our own necessary action. That's the man with the musket, eh, Ptah?"

"It is. His name is Henny Lagle, and he is the best marksman in all of Prussia."

"Good, good, good. Henny is about to lose his aim."

"And four shall become three."

"Oh, my God! Henny!" cried out Indra. "Henny! Let go!"

"Scare bleu!" gasped Andrew. "His flesh..!"

A searing nimbus haloed and shook the Prussian and stole the voice from his open mouth as it cooked him from the inside out, melting away his nose and tongue and lips. Chunks of the flesh dripped from his cheeks and jaw in bloody dollops onto his chest, eating away the flesh from the bones of his fingers.

"Don't touch him!" Rajesh yelled and turned to Andrew, extending his right arm. "Sir! Your crook! Now!"

And as the cloud of gas hissed and spewed and began to fill the Atlantean room, Rajesh covered his mouth with his left hand, seized Andrew's crook, and jerked back around to face the Prussian.

He stretched out the Shepard's staff and caught Henny by his neck in its hook.

"Got...to...pull..." he muttered, "uh."

And the captain of the Nautilus yanked Henny's fleshless hands off of the book and his charring body back from the podium. Henny's charred, jerking body fell back onto the floor, scattering cloudy waves of gas until his spasms died and Henny lay still.

Through the parted fingers covering his mouth, Singh said, "What did the..."

"No time!" yelled Rajesh, cutting Indra's words short. "Get out! Now! Follow me! Through the mirror! Hurry!"

Singh and Andrew stepped through the maw created by the shattered mirror.

"But, what of M'sieu Henny?" asked the Frenchman through the parted fingers covering his own mouth. "Is there nothing...?"

"What of Herr Henny?" barked Rajesh over the increasing roar of the hissing gas. "He is dead."

In an instant, the three men found themselves beyond the shattered mirror and standing in a base of a dimly lit, vertical shaft, their ankles already engulfed in swirling waves of poisonous gas.

"We are trapped," said Indra Singh. "Master, there is no escape from this."

"First the Chops, then Henny. We are dead men," said Andrew and looked up the shaft at a stronger light above them. "There is an opening above!"

Rajesh followed the direction of the Frenchman's gaze to a rectangular hole in the ceiling above them and a series of metal rungs in the shaft's wall that rose into the aperture and disappeared into its dim recess. Far above them in the shaft was a tiny rectangle of light.

He yelled over the hiss of the gas, "Then reason dictates we climb, sirs."

Without hesitation, Dakkar seized the lowest rung embedded in the wall with his left hand to ascend, as, in the same instant, Andrew grabbed his right forearm, almost jerking the Shepherd's Crook from his captain's right hand.

"Your stupid 'reason' have already killed three," snarled the Frenchman. "I think not I will be the four. Give me the crook. I will find another way out."

"Methane is lethal, M'sieu Andrew," said Rajesh. "Stay and die. There is no other way out."

Rajesh jerked his forearm free from Andrew's grip.

"It will kill you whether I am a fool or not. But do what you want."

"Ma foi," said the Frenchman through the fingers over his mouth and nose as he first looked down at the rising clouds of gas at his feet, then back through the shattered mirror at Henny's corpse, already almost completely submerged by the poison. "We are dead men, for sure."

Even before Andrew's prophecy, Rajesh's right leg alone remained visible as his captain ascended the rungs and Singh, with a hand on the first iron crosspiece, turned to speak to the confused and defeated Frenchman.

"As long as we draw breath," Singh advised, "there is hope, my friend." He dropped his hand from the rung, and pressed his palms together in an attitude of prayer. He bowed his head and smiled. Then the Indian turned from the Frenchman and to begin to climb the rung.

"Hope?" interrupted Andrew. "The hope of slow torture or quick death…"

Singh paused in his ascent and looked down at Andrew, "If you stay, you *will* fulfill your prophecy. Follow us, and you may live. The only guarantee is death if you remain, Andrew."

Singh's head and shoulders disappeared in the aperture in the ceiling as Andrew looked around the base of the shaft and the cloud of gas now swirling around his thighs.

Legrand turned and placed a hand on an embedded rung, and shrugged his shoulders.

"Hope," he said, "she springs eternal."

Chapter Sixteen

Andrew's head and shoulders disappeared into the vertical shaft in the room behind the shattered mirror in the Atlantis room as the cloud of poisonous gas filled half of the chamber. A bird hovering overhead might have mistaken him, Rajesh, and Singh for worms crawling up out of a narrow hole as the three men slowly ascended the rungs.

"The Chops and Henny died," Rajesh continued as he climbed, "because they ignored my directions, M'seiu Legrand. The Soters killed them, not my poor judgment. Unless you accept that, we have no chance to escape and all of our bones will join the ancient bones stored in this library."

"I have abandoned my search for the secret I sought. It is now to escape that must direct our every thought and movement. Anything less jeopardizes each of our lives."

Rajesh paused on a rung at a small mirror ratcheted just above him onto the wall next to a burning torch. The highly polished surface of the mirror had been positioned to direct light up and down the shaft. Dakkar twisted the mirror on its hinge to point it towards the wall.

"Another damned mirror," he said more to himself than to his fellow adventurers. "They have been monitoring our every move. This shaft must lead to a viewing room."

He began to ascend again as he added, "I doubt Nechops expected us to survive the gas or find this shaft. Therefore, it is unlikely there are traps in this passage, but who knows what waits for us at any turn."

The captain of the Nautilus paused at a landing near the top of the shaft, lifted his head above the level of its floor, and saw a cramped, horizontal corridor stretching to his left and right sides. The walls were embedded with the same torches that shed a dim light throughout the passageways of the Library of Alexandria.

"Sirs," he said as he stepped up onto the landing, "we have a chance to escape." He waited on the landing, holding Andrew's Sheppard's Crook, as first Singh and then the Frenchman joined him.

"Unless M'sieu Nechops waits in ambush, non?" said the swordsman. "There seems to be a booby trap at every other footstep and around every corner, my friend."

"We have no other option," responded Rajesh as he surveyed the passage opening before them. "Without the proper equipment, the twins and Herr Henn...Singh! Where is Olaf?"

Singh offered his upraised palms to indicate ignorance. "Master, in the confusion..."

"He was not in the Atlantis room, captain. If he falls behind," interjected the Frenchman, "he's maybe cut off by the slab that sealed the room, M'sieu."

Waving his two remaining Black Knights forward toward a door at the end of the corridor, Rajesh said, "Then you both are as rich as Midas, eh, M'sieu Andrew?"

"Wha the hell...!" the Frenchman cursed.

As they proceeded down the passage, Singh studied the burning torches on his right and left with a new and, considering their circumstances, misguided interest. Halfway down the hall, he said, "I didn't notice before, Rajesh, but none of the torches we've passed have been burned down to any degree. They must change the things constantly."

Rajesh's smile was whimsical. "As if this were the time or place to discuss such things, Singh. Not true, my friend. I noticed that early on. Look."

Rajesh stopped and thrust his hand into the flame of a torch.

Singh lurched forward to jerk his arm away as Rajesh smiled.

"My hand doesn't burn, my dear tutor because this is not a flame."

"Sacre Bleu!" gasped Andrew as he took Rajesh's hand and turned it over and back again to examine it. "What is this? It does not burn!"

"I have no explanation, Andrew. It is not fire, as you now surmise, and the wood of these torches is not consumed by 'flame'. What it is...is a total mystery to me, and one I sorely would like to unravel. But it does tell me that, in some things, the Soters have unraveled some of the mysteries held in the ancient documents that fill this library, and in others, their science is quite primitive. I have also deduced that the stone slabs that have opened for us and shut on us were moved by the power of steam. But I have seen no evidence that the Soters have mastered an advanced use of that power. Enough. Quickly now. We must find our way out."

Having arrived at the closed door at the end of the passage, Rajesh placed the head of the crook of the Shepard's staff against its surface.

"Stand a bit back, sirs," he said, and cautiously pushed against the door. "And wait a moment."

The door soundlessly swung open on hidden hinges revealing a small room with a golden pedestal in its center topped by a huge mirror and a chair facing it.

"Ingenious. It appears," said Rajesh, "that this must be one of the chambers from which Nechops and his cronies have been watching us."

Indra stood next to Dakkar surveying the area as Andrew's head appeared behind him in the opening in the door. To their left side were two closed doors and a cluster of rectangular blocks protruding irregularly out of the wall between these doors.

"Amazing!" said Captain Dakkar without crossing the threshold. "These caverns must be honeycombed with mirrors. But Nechops' grasp of science is limited and primitive."

"You are the cold bloodied fish, Dakkar," grumbled the Frenchman." What of Olaf? Remember? At least he may still live. Shouldn't we search for my little man?"

"If our situations were reversed," answered Rajesh, "would Mr. Templeton risk his life for us? I think not. Follow me, sirs."

Rajesh led Singh and Andrew deeper into the room, and immediately walked to the wall of rectangular blocks set in it at different depths to examine it.

"Look, Singh," he observed as he touched one of the blocks. "Everything is done by simple leverage. These walls must be honeycombed with tubing that carries steam from a central boiler to open, close, or move whatever Nechops wishes. Singh, Andrew, please examine the mirror."

"Master!" said Indra as he and the Frenchman moved to the pedestal. "Andrew is right. There is a time for scientific curiosity and observation. I am certain that this is not it."

"Olaf's miserable life is worth more than all thee knowledge in this stinking trap. We go back."

Rajesh pointed at the mirror with his left index finger.

"Please tilt the glass, M'sieu Andrew. Although it appears to be a simple mirror, I suspect it is much more, created somehow to not only project an image, but to receive one as well, and sometimes with the capability of receiving and broadcasting sound. The mechanism to accomplish these things must somehow be embedded in the mirror. As for Andrew's concerns about Olaf and our lives..."

"We may discover an exit using Nechops' system of mirrors that he uses for spying. As for Mr. Templeton's worth...if he has already looted the library, you may be right."

"What is this slander?" Legrand said as he began to try to turn the mirror, first by grasping its edges, and then by twisting its base. As the mirror slowly turned, Rajesh studied the changing images that flickered on its highly polished surface almost faster that he could discern them.

"Your sincere concern touches me, M'seiu Legrand. Is this what is meant by 'honor among thieves?'"

Abruptly, Nechops' grinning face materialized on the mirror.

"Singh!!" Rajesh shouted, leaning forward in Nechops' chair.

"Dakkar!" sneered Nechops from the mirror.

"Our game of chess is over, captain," said the Soter as a hooded figure appeared behind him. "You have misjudged your every move and lost every pawn. You lost even the first move in Delhi."

"Sacre Bleu!" exclaimed the Frenchmen as he leaned down to look at the Soter's face in the mirror. "We are discovered!"

The enigmatic figure behind Nechops pushed back its hood to pool around its shoulders, revealing the beautiful, chestnut-brown face of Soma.

"May I introduce my daughter," said Nechops. "The 'traitor' that you trusted with your life and the lives of your Black Knights in Delhi? Checkmate."

Singh pointed at the mirror as Andrew stepped away in disgust. "She sold you the map! It's the woman in Delhi!"

Rajesh jumped up from Nechops' chair and snatched the Shepherd's Crook from its resting place. His face red with humiliation and anger, he tossed the staff to Singh who caught it.

"Singh! SMASH IT! Smash the mirror!" he yelled.

Indra swung the Shepherd's Crook back and to his right side. Dakkar and Andrew covered their faces with their forearms as the Indian said, "So be it," and smashed the mirror into a shower of silver shards that rained, tinkling, to the stone floor.

At that instant, Andrew bolted for the wall of protruding stone blocks and the door to the right side of the death triggers.

"Andrew!" shouted Rajesh and loped after the swordsman. "Andrew! Stop! I was wrong about eluding Nechops!"

"Non? When have you ever been right, M'sieu," said Andrew as, using his arms like battering rams, he shoved the door open. "Ah, at last it is the freedom!"

"I could be wrong about traps!" Dakkar barked as he reached the Black Knight and grabbed Andrew's right forearm with his right hand. "I beg of you, don't do this!"

Andrew stopped in the threshold of the door to turn his attention to the small chamber before him. It had been chiseled from a fissure in the cave and finished with beige tiles on its walls and a flagstone floor in a jigsaw pattern. The chamber was dimly lit with faux burning torches. Another closed door was set in its opposite wall.

"The first step," said his captain, still clutching his forearm, "could mean instant death!"

"Viv la morte," sneered the Frenchman as he wrenched his arm free. "I am the patsy for your madness no more, 'captain'. If it pleases you...if I die, it will be by my own choices now. Au revoir."

"There are options," said Rajesh as Singh joined him. "There are always options. If we look, we will find them!"

"The time for talk is past," answered the French Black Knight as he gingerly paced a foot on the closest flagstone. "I have never feared death. I prefer to choose the time and the place."

"I may have need of the crook," Rajesh said and took the Shepherd's Crook from Singh as he continued to try to dissuade Andrew.

"Do you feel the intense heat, M'sieu Andrew? Those flagstones could cover a lava pit!"

"Better to burn in hell with Olaf than spend another moment under your thumb, M'sieu." He added his weight to his foot on the flagstone. The stone held.

"Andrew!" pleaded Rajesh, "please wait!"

Andrew turned to Dakkar's voice as he took his second guarded step into the room.

"The flagstones! If they crumble beneath....here!" Rajesh threw the Frenchman the Shepherd's Crook.

"Oui," Andrew said as he caught it, then turned his attention back to the jigsaw pattern of the floor. He continued to cautiously step across the flagstones one at a time using the crook to test each one as he moved towards the closed door on the opposite side of the chamber.

From the threshold of the entrance, Rajesh said, "M'sieu Andrew...shift your weight to..."

"Sahib!" interrupted Singh, placing a restraining hand on Dakkar's left arm. "Your outburst may kill him! Let him think."

Except for his tapping, an eerie silence seemed to blanket the room as Legrand, now two thirds of the way across the area, tested another stone with his crook and with the toe of his boot. It creaked beneath his weight. Andrew bit his lower lip, his face covered with beads of sweat, and stepped up to the threshold of the closed door. He raised his left hand and wiped the sweat from his eyes.

"Voila!" he said, raising his arms triumphantly and sharing a grin with Rajesh, who was scratching his head in consternation, and Singh, who returned the Frenchman's victorious smile.

"Freedom is near, oui?"

Andrew turned, grabbed its doorknob, and pulled the door open towards him.

Two, heavily bearded, hooded Soter thugs stood on the opposite side of the threshold.

Instantly, one threw his right arm around Andrew's shoulder and his left under the swordsman's left armpit. In the thug's left hand was a short sword. Its point found the base of Andrew's neck.

"The slightest movement," the thug snarled, "and you die."

"Oui, M'sieu Soter, I am the statue."

The second Soter snatched Andrew's crook from the Frenchman's hand.

Singh instinctively lunged forward into the room until Rajesh threw up a restraining arm; his accompanying look stopping his mentor dead in his tracks.

"I am called Ptah. You...Dakkar and your lackey," yelled the thug with the sword, "surrender now or your giant will gag on his own blood!"

Glaring at his fellow Soter, Ptah added, "Abantes. Destroy his crook."

"By your command, Lord Ptah."

Obediently, Abantes swung Andrew's crook with all of his strength against the wall. He cried out as if dropping a hot brand, let the vibrating staff fall from his stunned hands to the floor.

Abantes looked down at his stung, open palms, and whispered, "The damned thing is made of metal, Ptah!"

As he spoke, a third, clean-shaven, hooded Soter joined Ptah in the threshold of the doorway as Ptah restrained Andrew and barked at Rajesh and Singh.

"It changes nothing, you sniveling fools. The entrance behind you is locked. You cannot break it down. You cannot open it. You are trapped, without hope of escape. You are my prisoners. Surrender, now, or this miserable fool," he sneered, drawing his sword partially up and down Andrew's neck as if he were slitting the Frenchman's throat, "this one dies like the mongrel that he is."

Singh turned to test the doorknob in the door behind them, but was restrained by Rajesh's right hand on his right forearm. "No, Singh. Not now. We couldn't abandon Andrew," whispered Rajesh, "even if the door were already open."

"Then we are surely undone, my Prince."

"Indra, their presence may be our salvation," Rajesh whispered. "We must do as Ptah and his flunkies command. Think. We have escaped their maze of traps or Nechops would not intervene now to seal our fates. Come."

As they obeyed and began to cross the flagstones, Rajesh put his right hand into the right pocket of his pants.

"And I am not without a trick or five myself," he said as an aside to himself.

But his look of guarded confidence was replaced with consternation when he removed his hand and opened his palm on...nothing.

"The orbs!" he hissed. "My explosives! They're gone! But what could have..."

Rajesh's face flushed with cold anger as he spat, "Olaf!"

"You've brought chaos to an ordered brotherhood, Dakkar," Ptah said from the doorway. "You've left debris and dead bodies everywhere behind you wherever you've traveled. We cannot have that. Abantes, keep that sword on the one they call Andrew."

Ptah released Andrew, handed his sword to Eurydemos, and pushed the hood back from his head to pool around his shoulders.

"I would have the Shepherd's Crook, Abantes," commanded Ptah.

Abantes gave him Andrews' crook and pushed his own hood back from his head.

Eurydemos shook his head free of its covering and shoved Andrew several steps back into the room. He then followed Ptah, Abantes, and the Frenchman into the chamber.

As Rajesh and Singh approached them all, Ptah stopped at the wall on his left side and touched the palm of his free, left hand flat against it. He pushed, and the stone beneath his hand partially sank into the wall.

"I can't wait to take this sword and shove it," snarled Eurydemos raising his sword level with his chest, "up his a..."

"Enough!" snapped Ptah. "Save your obscenities for your boyfriends. But you can run that sword through Andrew if he so much as moves a muscle."

The stone beneath Ptah's hand struck an unseen stop in the wall. Suddenly, the crack of crumbling stone violated the silence as the floor between the Soter's and Rajesh and Singh blistered up and then began to fall apart, flagstone by flagstone, like a jigsaw puzzle being shaken asunder, creating a glowing crevice in the floor.

Rajesh and Singh watched as the red mouth widened and a gust of searing heat and fetid air rose from a pit of bubbling, white-hot lava that had been hidden beneath the floor. They stumbled back from the pit, covering their mouths and noses with their forearms, as Ptah raised the Shepherd's Staff, stepped gingerly to the edge of the blistering aperture, and raised it in his left hand over the maw.

"Three of our brothers have died because of you," Ptah said as flagstone after flagstone and the braces that supported them continued to collapse and fall into the lava. "All of you are the same. In your blind pursuit of knowledge, all you've found is your own stupidity."

He dropped the crook into the searing lava.

"For what you steal is neither good nor bad, Dakkar. It's your kind who misuse or pervert the scraps of truth stored in the library. We don't protect the library from the world, as you think. We protect the world from what the library holds."

"Sacre Bleu!" Andrew whispered, his eyes dilated with fear as he looked down into the random pattern of air bubbles that scabbed the lava and rose and burst and rose and burst. "That Indian pig was right about the lava!"

The Shepherd's Crook hit the boiling surface of the white-hot lava and an eruption of grey smoke moiled up through the maw. It began to smoke and melt as it sank.

"Of a certainty," continued Ptah as he lowered his arm, "what cures can also kill. We cannot allow the death in these volumes to spread. Especially the secret held in the manuscript you seek, Dakkar. The flagstones still standing around the open pit will not collapse. Walk around the maw to me. Do it now!"

Eurydemos pricked Andrew's back with the sword.

"Zut!" the Frenchman yelped and jerked away. A spot of blood began to spread beneath his black shirt on his back between his shoulder blades.

Ptah lowered his head, his eyes ablaze with an unholy light. "I...said... now!"

Rajesh and Singh gingerly skirted the gaping hole in the floor.

"Do not hurt one hair of Andrew's head, Ptah," Rajesh threatened, his eyes never leaving the lip of the remaining flagstones. "Or with God as my witness, you will pay dearly."

Ptah chuckled as Singh and Rajesh approached him. "Your stupidity is only trumped by your gigantic ego, Rajesh Dakkar, Prince of Bundlekund. I guess I should expect no less from a pampered, spoon-fed idiot of wealth and privilege."

Rajesh and Singh stopped in front of the grinning Soter with their faces blank, their rage repressed. Ptah jerked his head to his left indicating to both that they should proceed in front of the Soters and Andrew through the open door into the passageway behind them all. As he obeyed, Rajesh's slitted eyes never left Eurydemos as the captain of the Nautilus reached out and gingerly touched the spot of blood on Andrew's shirt.

"You will pay for this," he said at Eurydemos. "And for the men you killed today."

"Shut up, fool," snapped Ptah. "You will do nothing to Eurydemos or my brother or me. You are powerless before us. And you won't leave

Alexandria with the Atlantian manuscript wrapped around your forearm underneath your shirt either, Dakkar."

Singh's eyes widened in surprise as he turned to his master.

Rajesh's face remained blank.

"Zut!" Legrand said. "We are surely dead men."

The mirror attached to the back of Soma's vanity reflected her beautiful, eighteen-year-old, chestnut-brown face, large, blue, almond-shaped eyes, and a comely nose. Her lips were full and her forehead unblemished beneath a wealth of thick, black hair. She wore a simple, white, cotton robe cinched at the waist with a yellow cotton belt.

It was a face few people had ever seen or admired outside of the library.

Those eyes were full of a long-suffering, hopeless sadness that had yet to add a wrinkle to that face. The back of her right hand laying at the base of her neck was tattooed with the Soter open eye with an Ankh centered in its pupil. With her left hand, she mechanically combed her long hair.

Also reflected in the mirror behind the daughter of the Most Exalted High Custodian of the Library of Alexandria was the small bedroom where she had resided for a good deal of a claustrophobic life, captive in a dim world dominated by old men and vague memories of a mother who had died a terrible, slow death when she was seven years old. Those old men had been unable to find anything in their treasured, ancient documents that could save her mother, or the compassion to find anyone above ground who might have been able to do so.

Years, earlier, Soma had knelt by her mother's bed in this same room, sobbing, as her mother drew her last breath. Her father had stood by Soma with his hand on her shoulder. As was expected of the High Custodian, he had shed no tear. Most Exalted High Custodians do not cry.

On the top of her vanity lay a cluster of combs, brushes, jars, a small hand-held mirror with a turtle-shell back, tweezers, a scrap of paper, an open ink well, and a quill pen. Next to these items was a pair of flesh colored gloves. The jars held blacking for her eyelashes, rouge for her cheeks, a red dye for her lips, and a cream to remove it all at the end of the each day.

Outside of the few trinkets and modest pieces of art that hung on the stone walls of her bedroom bought during the rare trips allowed her above ground, they were the only things feminine now in a library that weren't centuries dead.

Soma laid her comb down on the vanity next to the scrap of paper, and picked up a jar. She opened its lid, and picking up one of the brushes, carefully and sparingly applied an artificial blush to her cheeks. She began to cry without sound.

By the left side of her vanity on the floor was a small, packed, cloth valise.

When she was finished with it, the young girl put the lid back on the jar of rouge, and picked up the jar of blacking that she used to darken and lengthen her eyelashes. She picked up a very small, circular brush. It took some time to apply the blacking; her hand shook at bit and she continued to cry. When she was finished, Soma dropped the tiny brush back on the vanity and put the lid back on the jar of blacking. It was a routine made mindless by endless routine.

She could do so almost instinctively because she had added these cosmetics to make her at least look like a woman, although she knew that she really wasn't, really, a woman, for at least five years, maybe longer.

Her emotions overwhelmed her then, and she laid her head on the backs of her hands on the vanity and sobbed and shook for a long time. But even the wailing at a funeral finally ends; she knew because she had eventually stopped weeping after her mother's funeral. So she lifted her head, and wiped away the last vestiges of tears from her eyes with the heels of her hands. Then she picked up her gloves from the vanity, and put them on, covering the Soter open eye with an Ankh centered in its pupil on her right hand.

Soma pushed her chair back and rose from the vanity. She stooped and picked up the valise, then walked to the closed bedroom door, opened it, and stopped in its threshold.

She looked back at the room where she had spent almost eighteen years of her lonely, isolated life. She thought of her father, Nechops, and that she would never see him again. She thought of her mother's grave, hidden deep in the caverns of the library, and that she'd never lay flowers on it again. Then she thought of the boys above ground that she'd never met, never dated, never kissed, of the girlfriend's she'd never had, of the silly gossip she'd never shared with a girlfriend, of a first love she'd never felt, of dances, and dresses, and ribbons for her hair, of dolls, and presents, and frilly dresses and birthday parties with friends her own age, and the things that girls buy, and of the movement she had never felt in her womb.

Then Soma walked through the door to her bedroom and closed it quietly behind her.

She walked down the secret hall that, enlarged and carved from one of the hundreds of natural fissures in the caverns, slowly rose up and led to a secret door that opened onto the city of Alexandria, a city almost wholly unknown to her.

When she arrived at that door, she took out a key and opened it. It opened onto an alley that led to the same boulevard that Dakkar and the Black Knights had traveled to reach the Library. She turned, threw the key back into the passageway, and closed the door. It locked itself behind her.

She walked down the boulevard, weaving in and out of the flow of people she did not know, into a future she could not imagine, eventually disappearing into the crowd.

She never looked back.

The message in her handwriting on the scrap of paper laying on her vanity read:

Murderer.

Chapter Seventeen

His hood pooled around his neck, Ptah stood in the mouth of the dark passageway and said, "The place of the cure of the soul."

He stood at the head of a cluster of hooded Soters, three with spears, who surrounded Andrew, Singh, and Rajesh. Andrew's jaw hung open in astonishment. Rajesh stood emotionally indifferent next to Singh as Andrew said, "Oui. It smells like dead fish that were sick."

"You smell the petroleum," Rajesh said, cupping his chin with the fingers of his right hand, "seeping from every crevice, M'sieu Andrew, and something else that stinks..."

"Nechops," said Singh.

Before them, under the toothed dome of a huge cavern towering over thirty feet above their heads and studded by random clusters of stalactites bedded in shadows, lay a small lake infested with sluggish crocodiles. To their left side, the lake lapped up against a peninsula of rock. On the floor of that peninsula, a flurry of stone steps in its center lead up to an ornate dais and a raised throne of gold topped by the open eye with an Ankh centered in its pupil that was duplicated on Nechops' forehead.

Nechops sat on the elaborately carved throne that was flanked with two golden blazers on slim, ten-foot-tall poles, eying them like a hawk watching a rat. His fingers were intertwined into a cathedral touching his chin. Flanking the Curator and on rising steps at both sides of the dais, stood six immobile Soters armed with spears and swords. They, in turn, were also flanked by a row of three golden blazers on thick pedestals.

"Surprise, surprise, surprise," groused Andrew, "there are more than seven or eight Soters."

His guard punched Andrew in the ribs with the butt of his sword.

Behind the contingent of guards to the right side of Nechops' throne, a statue of the Egyptian bird-god, Ibis, towered twelve feet into the close, smarmy air. The god's beak was open and a small waterfall flowed out of it and splashed into a channel cut in the stone floor that emptied the water into the lake. The walls were everywhere covered with the blazing faux torches that were not consumed.

His cathedral of fingers parted, and Nechops' uncalloused right hand touched an almost invisible stud in the arm of the throne. Once again, deep within the bowels of the library, steam churned and rushed up through a web of tubes in the stone walls of the cavern, hissing through substations to their final destination, and a stone slab fell to seal the passage behind the Black Knights and their guards.

"Move," Ptah ordered his prisoners. "Nechops is impatient with his servant."

The three hooded thugs behind Andrew, Singh, and Rajesh prodded them with their spears.

Andrew turned to scowl at his guard. "The squirrel awaits his nut, non?"

The guard jabbed him into motion with the butt of his spear.

As guards and prisoners alike approached the foot of the dais, Nechops rose from his throne with a cocky smile on his bronze face and slowly descended the dais steps to meet Andrew, Singh, and Rajesh and their guards.

"So this is the 'god.'" said Rajesh, "who withholds the knowledge that would free mankind."

As he spoke, Rajesh began to reach into the right sleeve of his shirt with his left hand.

Nechops raised his left hand and snapped his fingers, and Rajesh's guard stepped quickly around the captain of the Nautilus to the side of the Custodian.

"I waste no time on children," said Nechops, lowering his arm. "I want the Atlantean manuscript you stole from me earlier, Dakkar."

His words as hard and cold as ice, Rajesh said, "When Hell freezes over."

Nechops nodded at the hooded Soter standing at his left side. Without

"Move! Nechops is impatient with his servant."

warning, the guard took three steps forward, drew back his spear, and thrust it in Andrew's stomach!

"Andrew!" Rajesh shouted and lunged forward, his face distorted by horror and surprise.

"'hulck guk," Andrew's spat through the blood foaming up and through his throat and into his mouth. The Frenchman hunched forward, clutching the shaft of the spear imbedded in his midriff, fell to his knees, and then collapsed backward to the floor on his back, dead.

"And then there were only two too many," said Nechops.

"I'll kill you!" Rajesh yelled.

Wild with anger and balling his hands into fists, he hurled himself at Nechops.

"I'll kill...!"

"Sahib! Stop it! Stop!" Singh grabbed his master by his right arm and pulled him, struggling, back from Nechops.

"You bastard! Why did you kill him?" Rajesh snarled, his rage raw, his eyes filled with tears. "I offered no resistance!"

"Little Prince," grinned Nechops, "you still know nothing of people. It is your greatest weakness, so I use it. I did so..."

Nechops kicked Andrew's dead body in the ribs.

"...because I can."

"As I live and breathe," Rajesh threatened, "you will never leave this place alive, Nechops."

"Really," said Nechops, and kicked Andrew's corpse in the ribs with such force that the Frenchman began to roll over and was stopped only by the wooden shaft of the spear protruding from the growing stain of blood at his belly.

Rajesh's eyes burned with fire. He clenched his teeth as he turned his head away from the grisly sight as his fingernails cut tiny half-moons of blood into the palms of his clenched fists. Singh buried his face in his raised right hand and prayed.

Nechops waved two of his thugs forward. "Our gentle pets look hungry. Feed them."

Two guards picked up Andrew's corpse by the shoulders and legs and carried it to the edge of the peninsula. Without ceremony, they began to swing the Frenchman back and forth until, at the height of a forward thrust, they released his body.

"Andrew," Rajesh whispered.

There was a splash. There was a second and then a third, distant splash.

There was a furious thrashing in the lake where Andrew's body had been thrown.

Then there was no sound at the edge of the peninsula except the shuffle of the Soters as they returned to the side of their master.

"Well...." said Nechops. "The manuscript?"

Rajesh jerked his arm free of Singh's restraining grip, angry but now in control of himself. Supremely confident, Nechops held out his right hand to receive the manuscript as Rajesh reached into the right sleeve of his black shirt with his left hand...and hesitated.

"Whether you surrender it," Nechops sneered, "or I pry it from your dead fingers, the manuscript is mine. Only this choice is left you, 'Prince' Dakkar, you who are the apex of human perfection, superior to everyone in every way, faster, stronger, smarter, move vital and full of life than any other man."

Nechops laughed derisively. "Sniveling fool."

Rajesh pulled out one of two manuscripts lying one against the other that were wrapped around his forearm and, therefore, hidden from Nechops by his shirt sleeve. Without looking at the library's curator, he scratched the surface of the manuscript with a fingernail as he extended it to Nechops.

"Master," whispered Singh and dropped his hand from his anguished face.

"Even that choice will not change your fate," said Nechops as he stepped forward to accept the offered document. "The only question is: which one of you shall die first, the prince of fools or..."

"As you say," Rajesh interrupted. He turned his dead, emotionless face back to Nechops. "Which will die first."

"For myself," continued the Soter, "the expression on your face as a crocodile disembowels your manservant who...what...?"

Nechops looked down at his hand as the manuscript burst into flames.

"The answer?" said Rajesh. "You die first."

"My robe!" screamed Nechops as he dropped the burning manuscript and a river of fire crawled up his sleeve and his flesh began to burn, sizzle, and crackle. "My ROBE! I'm on fire—! Help me!"

His thugs around him recoiled with surprise and horror. Abantes yelled, "Nechops! Your arm!?!" and the clutch of Soters instinctively drew back as Nechops screamed beating with his hands at the roaring flames that were engulfing him.

"Singh! Follow my lead!" yelled Rajesh.

"Allow me," he added in the same breath as he crossed his forearms before his lowered head and, using his full body weight in his charge, threw himself like a living ram against the fiery mass of the barely living body of the High Custodian of the Library of Alexandria.

Rajesh fell back from Nechops and onto his butt and watched Nechops' body toppled back and splash into the lake in a geyser of flames, heard several distant splashes joined the first and became a great reptilian thrashing, saw the surface of the lake erupt into a sheet of flame, and the guards of the Alexandrian Library turned in horror and fled in every direction.

As the flames on the lake spread and roared into an inferno and crocodiles dived to escape death, Rajesh stood up.

He raised his left to his right knee, began to remove his boot, and shouted, "Off with them, Singh, and dive!"

Rajesh ran to the edge of the subterranean lake.

"Dive, sahib?!?" Singh asked as he watched his student, his friend, his captain, dive into the raging flames.

Nemo laid his quill pen down on his desk and looked at what he had written in his diary. Then he took up the pen to write again.

Singh never knew I had placed the real Atlantean manuscript in a second, airtight pouch beneath my sleeve. That a second, fake "manuscript" on top of it was chemically treated to burst into flame at contact with the air. At least one thing that I'd anticipated and preplanned to prevent on that terrible day had worked.

He must have also thought diving into a sheet of burning oil that covered the surface of the underground lake was pure madness.

He was ignorant of what I had deduced. That an outlet for the lake had to exist somewhere beneath that flaming surface.

He was a man of wisdom, not science.

Singh was famous for his mastery of philosophy, religion and literature, and for his unfailing love of India. Like my father, he believed his long degraded and heathen country would someday rise to the same enlightened level of most of the nations of Europe.

I believed they had labored long and hard to groom me from birth as an instrument to that end. I believed Singh's unflinching loyalty to me was rooted in that goal.

I was wrong.

Singh dived into the burning lake.

The force of his clean dive propelled the Indian through and beneath the blanket of fire and parallel to Rajesh's waist who, unaware of Indra's presence and with powerful strokes, was cleaving the murky water irrationally lit by a weird, dim phosphorescence. Despite Singh's own steady strokes, the Indian could not pull himself even with his captain.

It was then he saw the prehistoric horror.

Singh reached out and grabbed Rajesh's ankle, pulling him to a stop and jerking him upright to dog paddle next to him.

Maddened by the fire above, a crocodile, hurtled at them not ten feet away, its jaws closed but nevertheless the certain agency of a savage, bloody death, its muscled tail drubbing side to side in an eerie primeval rhythm.

Singh shoved Rajesh behind him and furiously waved his arms to distract the beast.

At five feet, the crocodile's jaws snapped open, flashing twin quarrels of razor-sharp teeth.

Singh twisted to one side of the path of the crocodile like a matador teasing a bull.

With incredible force, the crocodile struck him a glancing blow on his left shoulder, throwing him off-balance and back against Rajesh...and swam away.

Singh twisted around in the murky water to face Rajesh as his captain grinned sheepishly and wiped imaginary sweat from his brow. Then, following a direction indicated by Rajesh's pointed arm, both men dove down deeper until, in five quick strokes, they reached what Rajesh's had deduced must exist on the floor of the lake, a metal grate.

Rajesh's face expressed relief that he'd found what he sought.

As they dog paddled above the grate, they felt the tug of an incredibly strong, downward current and saw tiny bits of suspended debris being sucked down and through the grate. Epiphany lit Singh's face as he realized that Rajesh had dove into the fiery lake to find just such a point of necessary egress for the lake's mucky water. But a second's hope faded as he saw Rajesh's expression of hope change to black despair.

The grate covered an opening too small for escape for Singh.

In the uncanny silence, Rajesh and Indra exchanged momentary, unspoken looks of deep disappointment and then indecision as the air in their lungs continued to be depleted.

Rajesh shook his head to indicate the failure of his idea and pointed up to the surface of the lake with his right arm and index finger signaling that they must resurface or drown.

He partially squatted to push off from the floor of the lake with his legs. At the same moment, Singh braced both of his legs around the lip of the grating, seized it, and yanked it out of its moorings.

Diary.
Singh's faith overcame fear. He knew the answer to the question
that haunted my life. He had always known.
He knew the answer that I would not hear.
His loyalty was not based on my genius or India's needs.
He loved me.

Lungs crying out for air, Singh turned from the open egress, released his right hand, and seized Rajesh's right leg. Grabbing Rajesh's left forearm and pulling himself up, Singh rose to the level of his captain's face as he twisted Rajesh around to face him.

As they floated in the murky water, Rajesh's questioning look was met by Singh's expression of sadness, farewell, and unmistakable love; a moment frozen in time that wordlessly spoke of eighteen years of Singh's selfless dedication to his student, his dearest friend, and his captain, of a love greater than even self-preservation.

His cheeks ballooned with air, Singh raised his right hand, palm forward and gestured Rajesh to stop his ascent. Then, unexpectedly, he twisted Rajesh's right arm behind him.

As Dakkar realized what Singh was doing, he struggled in vain to free himself but he could not break free.

Indra quickly twisted Rajesh's left arm behind him and, restraining both of Dakkar's hands in his own left hand, grabbed Rajesh with his free hand by the nape of his neck.

He forced Rajesh, struggling, back down towards the grated, rectangular hole in the lake's floor.

He shoved Rajesh, head first, into the egress.

Singh turned his back on the man he loved and swam for the surface as Rajesh was sucked completely down by the current into a drainage pipe that was barely wider than his body.

As Indra swam up, he did not dwell on the sure death that awaited him at the hands of the Soters, nor did his life flash before his eyes, nor did me think of friends, family, or lovers, or of the joys and regrets of his life, or even on the pure light at the end of his earthly life that he knew would welcome him into the arms of God.

He thought about never seeing Rajesh again.

And as Singh rose in the lake, Rajesh hurtled like a bullet shot from the barrel of a musket, pulled along by the incredibly powerful undertow of water, his arms pinned to his sides and his cheeks ballooned with captured air. He fought with all of his remaining strength to remain conscious as his lungs began to empty of the last vestiges of air and his vision blurred and he became disoriented.

As Rajesh was flushed from the lake, Singh broke its surface in a fountain of water, gasping for air.

As his lungs filled, he began to dog paddle to stay afloat. He turned around as he bobbed on the surface of the lake, relieved to see the blanket of fire had completely burned itself out.

Singh finally turned to face the peninsula from which he had escaped only moments ago.

On the shore stood five very solemn and angry Soters, some with swords drawn and spears leveled. Still bobbing , Singh smiled and shook water from his bald pate and face. Then, paraphrasing the God he so loved, Singh said, "Forgive them, Lord.

"They know not what they do."

Diary.

I was eighteen and determined to lay bare the Great Secret at any cost. Singh knew the cost.

Singh knew the value of a man lies not in what he wins...but in what he is willing to lose.

God save my soul.

At the moment that Singh was praising God, Rajesh was spat out of the drainage pipe like a limp rag doll in an explosion of water.

Gasping for air and clutching desperately for purchase, Rajesh tumbled from the pipe projecting from an outcropping of stone into a narrow trench reinforced with mortared stones.

As he tumbled head over heels with the water in the trench and was deposited in the shallows of the ocean, he had but one thought.

I'm alive!

The Prince of Bundlekund struggled up from the shallow waters of the bay and, on his hands and knees, and near exhaustion, Rajesh Dakkar, Captain of the Nautilus and mankind's best hope for the future, crawled like a whipped dog onto the beach where he collapsed.

He lay still for a long time.

Then he sat up and turned his back on the ocean, sitting cross legged on the beach, soaked and filthy, swallowing great gulps of air to replenish his depleted lungs. When at last his lungs were refreshed, he began to survey his surroundings.

There was no obvious human development outside of the trench and the conduit in the outcropping behind him, so he reasoned the beach was unused for commerce, and that he was safe from discovery and the certainty of pursuit by the remaining Soters at least for a few minutes. He noted the handful of palm trees that stretched to the horizon to his left, and the otherwise cerulean blue sky that was spotted with random, sleepy white clouds above him.

Rajesh pulled the Atlantean manuscript from the watertight pouch sewed beneath his right sleeve and laid it on the sand in front of him. He reverently traced the letters in the language of the dead nation of the Atlanteans on its cover with the fingers of his right hand.

It read:

ⵀⴱⴰⵙ

It looked like Nemo, the Latin word for "no man" had been partially crushed.

The best hope of mankind began to weep.

Rajesh looked up from the cover of the manuscript, his face awash with tears, and sobbed.

The gulls that slowly rolled in the sky above him were indifferent. The sun did not noticeably sink deeper into the bay, and the waves lapping onto the beach did not join in his sorrow.

After some time, Rajesh rubbed the tears from his face with the heels of his hands. Then, slowly, he calmed himself and turned back around to face the ocean.

He did not know that his caste dot had been erased from his forehead.

Rajesh sat on the beach watching the sun on the edge of the horizon over the ocean. He welcomed the beautiful day that he had not made. Gnats that he did not create swirled around his face, and the palm trees that he did not design swayed gently in a breeze that he did not control.

And quietly, like the whisper of the waves that lapped close to his bare feet, Rajesh said to no one but himself, "I am no one. I have no nation. No family."

"From today and forever more, I am Nemo."

Epilogue

Captain Nemo sat at his desk bolted to the lurching floor of the Nautilus, the thumb of his right hand on his cheek and his remaining fingers cupping his chin. His face was calm but there were tears in his eyes as he looked at the picture of Singh that he held in his left hand.

From the disarray of memories in the small box on his desk, images of a mother cradling a very young boy, of a middle-aged man dressed as an Indian Rajah, of his mother, of Rajesh as a teenaged boy, he looked at the faded photograph that he had taken from the box of Singh dressed in the traditional robe of India called a lungis, standing in front of his fathers palace in Bundlekund.

He replaced the photograph back in the small box and turned his attention to his opened diary. He picked up his quill pen, dipped it in the ink well, and wrote.

My recent adventures with Cyrus Harding, Pencroft, Neb, and the castaways on the mysterious island where I had initially "come to die" are recounted elsewhere in this diary. But I feel compelled to record the whole truth now.

That the castaways found the Nautilus docked in the huge cavern beneath the island was no accident. That, as the sole survivor of the crew of the Nautilus, I had come to the island to die was, however, a lie.

I had not intended to die. Life plays dice with every man, and I will die now.

My command for the castaways to scuttle the Nautilus was also a ruse. Captain Harding and his castaways only thought they sank the Nautilus.

After they disembarked from my submarine, I ran my greatest creation out from the cavern into the turbulent waters that circle this island so that the bones of the Nautilus will never be found by anyone who might follow Harding's directions to her grave. He will tell someone. It is human nature. But the world is not ready for her magnificent secrets.

It is not lost on me that this is the same Soter philosophy that had withheld the incredible knowledge and the benefits of that knowledge from mankind for centuries; a belief that, at that time, I opposed and breached.

But I learned much from that expedition, and, in particular, from the too brief time I was allowed with Singh.

I knew that knowledge is power.

I learned that knowledge is not wisdom.

Singh me taught that knowledge is a sword with two edges, one reaps harvest and one destruction. It must be tempered with wisdom.

But I did not listen, and it was life that taught me that he was right. The Atlantean secrets I stole from the Soters that power this submarine did little to benefit the world under my hand. Someday, men will learn to temper knowledge with wisdom. Someday, men will be ready to harness the secrets of electricity, but not now. He taught me that right knowledge does not guarantee right choices. The complexities of life makes it impossible for any man, no matter what his education or how great his intellect, to know everything needed to make right choices in every situation. I lost too many men believing otherwise. And, finally but most importantly, I learned that there is a God, and that I am not He.

What I record now at the end of my time on earth may seem random, even disjointed or frivolous. But I write it nevertheless.

My hope, although not rational, is that Olaf somehow escaped the Library and lives somewhere today, happily picking the pockets of some unsuspecting victim.

I have no such hope for the greatest man I ever knew, Indra Singh.

How I escaped Egypt and returned to India will have to remain a mystery to whomever finds and reads this diary. There is no time to record that harrowing part of my life.

Nemo removed a waterproof strong box from a shelf, opened it, and placed his diary inside with the pictures that had lain on his desk. He closed and locked the strongbox with a key taken from one of his trouser pockets. Tucking the box under his right arm, he moved to the open doorway to his stateroom, and paused, framed by his beloved, massive pipe organ behind him, steadying himself against the ever increasing pitch of the submarine by placing his left hand on the doorjamb. He did not look back. He could not look back.

Then he walked purposefully down the lurching corridor to his stateroom, past the magnificent paintings, tapestries, religious icons, ancient fetishes, and gold artifacts that he had collected from the sunken treasure ships and lost cities forever buried on the floor of the ocean. He arrived at the closed, watertight door to one of the many vertical stairwells at the end of corridors that gave access to the multiple levels of the Nautilus. He turned the wheel in the center of the door; the quick opening mechanism that releases all of the latches called "dogs" around the periphery of a submarine's watertight door, opened it, and descended the stairwell.

A second hallway ornamented with fantastic treasures and then a stairwell, and a third corridor and stairwell finally brought him to the torpedo room in the bowels of the submarine. He went inside.

At the foot of the first of six torpedo tubes in the hull of the submarine sat several boxes and containers of different shapes and sizes where Nemo had originally secured them. He stopped at this tube and lay his strongbox down with the others, twisted the wheel that opened the hatch of the tube, and pushed it up on its hinges. Nemo methodically picked up and placed each of the containers in the empty breech, one at a time, often pausing to steady himself against the increasing list of the Nautilus, until all were inside the tube. Then he resealed the hatch.

He said to the precious cargo that the tube would spit into the ocean, "God speed."

Nemo pulled down the first of two large levers next to the tube that opened the external hatch of the torpedo tube. He waited a moment for it to fill with sea water. There was no need to aim its load; his target was anywhere away from the island and the submarine. So he pulled down the lever that had fired so many of the deadly accurate torpedoes that had sunk so many war ships, and listened to the familiar, accompanying whoosh of successful deployment. Nemo did not smile. He did not frown. He did not weep.

The watertight containers hurled away from the Nautilus and the island, leaving foaming trails in their wave, just thirty feet below the surface of the ocean.

With the reverence of placing a wreath on a grave, Nemo turned to the second large switch on the wall and pulled it down. The huge Atlantean dynamos of the Nautilus began to rev down until they fell silent. He did not move from the switch. He did not need to move.

It was then that the island arched its back like a man electrocuted as its twin volcanoes exploded a last time with unimaginable, profane fury, hurling great chucks of debris up to hang for an illusory instant in the air before raining fiery death down on every living thing below. It was then that the explosion huffed a massive burst of red-hot wind of hurricane strength that first bent and then tore up the island's trees and vegetation by their roots, and churned the already turbulent waters of the bay into an ever-widening whirlpool sucking everything in its path down to utter devastation in its bowels.

And the mighty Nautilus upended on the periphery of the hellish whirlpool to be, at first, sucked around and down, around and down, around and down, picking up dizzying speed in its hellish descent, around and down into the watery vortex of oblivion.

Until the submarine was no more.

Final entry. Diary of the Nautilus.

> *I have lived for sixty-six years, obsessed by an unquenchable thirst* for knowledge. I shall live no more.
>
> Many hailed me a genius. I debated with the greatest intellects of science. My wealth was immeasurable. The tomes of Alexandria's fabled Library have crumbled in my hands. Yet I die a man of no country or time, the most wretched and alone of men.
>
> It need not be so.
>
> *Read these words and take heed.*

As the blood-red sun sank beneath the horizon, the uber-violence of the whirlpool diminished, it's horrendous power depleted, and the twin volcanoes were no more, reduced to a great lake of burning slag, and the waves of the bay subsided and calmed.

All that remained of the mightiest power ever harnessed by man, the magnificent Nautilus, bobbed in an ocean turned into a filthy soup of debris, of shards of trees, the oily, bloated, mangled corpses of birds and animals, and tangled morasses of tropical plants and vegetation, was a random cluster of watertight boxes. On the lid of one of these was:

THE END

Appendix A

NEMO

by Jules Verne
from the novel The Mysterious Island

[Author's Note: I thought the reader might be interested in seeing how I took what Verne wrote about Nemo and added to it without violating the spirit of Verne's famous creation. Watch closely; the changes are sometimes subtle!]

Captain Nemo was an Indian, the Prince Dakkar, son of the Rajah of the then independent territory of Bundelkund. His father sent him, when ten years of age, to Europe, in order that he might receive an education in all respects complete, and in the hope that by his talents and knowledge he might one day take a leading part in raising his long degraded and heathen country to a level with the nations of Europe.

He traveled over the whole of Europe. His rank and fortune caused him to be everywhere sought after, but the pleasures of the world had for him no attractions. Though young and possessed of every personal advantage, he was ever grave—somber even—devoured by an unquenchable thirst for knowledge, and cherishing in the recesses of his heart the hope that he might become a great and powerful ruler of a free and enlightened people.

Still, for long the love of science triumphed over all other feelings. He became an artist deeply impressed by the marvels of art, a philosopher to whom no one of the higher sciences was unknown, a statesman versed in the policy of European courts. To the eyes of those who observed him superficially he might have passed for one of those cosmopolitans curious of knowledge but disdaining action; one of those opulent travelers, haughty and cynical, who move incessantly from place to place, and are of no country.

This artist, this philosopher, this man was, however, still cherishing the hope instilled into him from his earliest days.

Prince Dakkar returned to Bundelkund in the year 1848. ((His father's home/palace was on the banks of the Ganges near the city of Delhi.)) He married a noble Indian lady, who was imbued with an ambition not less ardent than that by which he was inspired. Two children were born to them, whom they tenderly loved. But domestic happiness did not prevent him from seeking to carry out the object at which he aimed. He waited an opportunity. At length, as he vainly fancied, it presented itself.

Instigated by princes equally ambitious and less sagacious, and more unscrupulous than he was, the people of India were persuaded that they might successfully rise against their English rulers, who had brought them out of a state of anarchy and constant warfare and misery, and had established peace and prosperity in their country. Their ignorance and gross superstition made them the facile tools of their designing chiefs.

In 1857 ((Nemo was 39 years old)) the great Sepoy revolt broke out. Prince Dakkar, under the belief that he should thereby have the opportunity of attaining the object of his long-cherished ambition, was easily drawn into it. He forthwith devoted his talents and wealth to the service of this cause. He aided it in person; he fought in the front ranks; he risked his life equally with the humblest of the wretched and misguided fanatics; he was ten times wounded in twenty engagements, seeking death but finding it not, when at length the sanguinary rebels were utterly defeated, and the atrocious mutiny was brought to an end.

Never before had the British power in India been exposed to such danger, and if, as they had hoped, the Sepoys had received assistance from without, the influence and supremacy in Asia of the United Kingdom would have been a thing of the past.

The name of Prince Dakkar was at that time well known. He had fought openly and without concealment. A price was set upon his head, but he managed to escape from his pursuers.

Civilization never recedes; the law of necessity ever forces it onward. The Sepoys were vanquished and the land of the Rajas of old fell again under the rule of England.

Prince Dakkar, unable to find that death he courted, returned to the mountain fastnesses of Bundelkund. There, alone in the world, overcome by disappointment at the destruction of all of his vain hopes, a prey to profound disgust for all human beings filled with hatred of the civilized world, he realized the wreck of his fortune, assembled some score of his most faithful companions, and one day disappeared, leaving no trace behind.

Where, then did he seek that liberty denied him upon the inhabited earth? Under the waves, in the depths of the ocean, where none could follow.

The warrior became the man of science. Upon a deserted island of the Pacific he established his dock-yard, and there a submarine vessel was constructed from his designs. *By methods which will at some future day be revealed, he had rendered subservient the illimitable forces of electricity,* which, extracted from inexhaustible sources, was employed for all the requirements of his floating equipage as a moving, lighting, and heating agent.* The sea, with its countless treasures, its myriads of fish, its numberless wrecks, its enormous mammalia, and not only all that nature supplied, but also all that man had lost in its depths, sufficed for every want of the prince and his crew—and thus was his most ardent desire accomplished, never again to hold communication with the earth. He named his submarine vessel the Nautilus, called himself simply Captain Nemo, and disappeared beneath the sea.

During many years this strange being visited every ocean from pole to pole. Outcast of the inhabited earth, in these unknown worlds he gathered incalculable treasures. The millions last in the Bay of Vigo, in 1702, by the galleons of Spain, furnished him with a mine of inexhaustible riches which he devoted always anonymously in favor of those nations who fought for the independence of their country (the insurrection of the Candiotes was largely assisted by Nemo).

For long, however, he had held no communication with his fellow-creatures [48 years old], when, during the night of the 6th of November, 1866, three men were cast on board his vessel. These three men had been hurled overboard by a collision which had taken place between the Nautilus and the United States frigate Abraham Lincoln, which had chased her.

Captain Nemo learned from this professor that the Nautilus, taken now for a gigantic mammal of the whale species, not for a submarine vessel carrying a crew of pirates, was sought for in every sea.

He might have returned these three men to the ocean, from whence chance had brought them in contact with this mysterious existence. Instead of doing this, he kept them prisoners, and during seven months they were enabled to behold all the wonders of a voyage of twenty thousand leagues under the seas.

One day, the 22nd of June, 1867, these three men, who knew nothing of the past history of Captain Nemo, succeeded in escaping in one of the Nautilus' boats. But as at this time the Nautilus was drawn into the vortex of the maelstrom, off the coast of Norway, the captain naturally believed that the fugitives, engulfed in that frightful whirlpool, found their death at the bottom of the abyss. He was ignorant that the Frenchman and his two companions had been miraculously cast on shore, that the fishermen of the Loffoden Islands had rendered them assistance, and that the professor, on his return to France, had published that work in which seven months of the strange and eventful navigation of the Nautilus were narrated and exposed to the curiosity of the public.

For a long time after this Captain Nemo continued to live thus, traversing every sea. But, one by one, his companions died, and found their last resting place in their cemetery of coral, the bed of the Pacific. At last, Captain Nemo remained the solitary survivor of all those who had taken refuge with him in the depths of the ocean.

He was now sixty years of age. Although alone, he succeeded in navigating the Nautilus toward one of those submarine caverns which had sometimes served him as a harbor.

One of these ports was hollowed beneath Lincoln Island, and at this moment furnished an asylum to the Nautilus.

[And, after six years beneath Lincoln Island, and at the climax of the book called *The Mysterious Island*, Nemo died at the age of 66. It was 1884.]

*This is where the premise of the novel you just read was gleaned.

***

This book is dedicated to:

Charles Wood, Larry Allison,
and James Copeland

Back Story

There are two stories behind the one you have just read.

The first story was written by Jules Gabriel Verne (8 February 1828 – 24 March 1905), who was a pioneer of Science Fiction. Among his many works, he created Captain Nemo (Prince Rajesh Dakkar) and wrote the novel *20,000 Leagues Under the Sea* that was first published in 1870 and has since become a classic of literature. Nemo would appear again under Verne's pen in the novel *The Mysterious Island* (1874). The writer's fictional inventor of the submarine has since become an icon of the genre that the French novelist helped to create, and the subject of several motion pictures, at least one television drama, and even of an animated series.

The second story began when Malibu Comics called me in late 1990 or early 1991. I had been writing comic strips and comic books for some time. In fact, I had created and co-authored an eight issue SF suspense-thriller with writer **R. A. Jones** called *Straw Men* that had been published by Innovation Press and drawn by artist **Rob Davis**. I've always suspected that R. A. Jones, who was a top writer for Malibu at the time, had recommended me to the publisher.

When Malibu called, an editor gave me a list of famous, public domain, fictional characters to choose from as the basis for a comic book title. I chose Nemo and decided to stay as true as possible to Verne's original vision of the character while writing a prequel to his famous novel.

In 1991, I wrote the three-issue comic book title, *The Adventures of Captain Nemo*. Comic book artist and Airship 27 Artistic Director **Rob Davis** was the artist on the title, and had actually drawn all three issues before the first issue was to be released. Then he had a dispute with Malibu and the project was abandoned.

After time passed, I submitted the mini-series in response to an advertisement in a trade publication from Rip Off Press soliciting ideas for new comic book series. They published the first issue of *Nemo* in 1992, then promptly went out of business.

In 2013, I submitted the idea to adapt that comic book mini-series into a novel to **Ron Fortier**, publisher of Airship 27. He accepted it and suggested Redbud, an affiliate of Airship 27 run by **Rob Davis,** publish the original comic book as a graphic novel at about the same time the novel would be released. I wrote the novel, and you hold **Young Nemo and The Black Knights** in your hands.

And it only took 24 years!

About Our Creators

AUTHOR

MICHAEL VANCE - was born in Oklahoma City, Oklahoma.

He was first published in "The Professor's Story Hour" chapbook at the age of eleven. He has been published in dozens of magazines and as a syndicated columnist and cartoonist in over 500 newspapers. His history book, *Forbidden Adventure, The History of the American Comics Group*, has been called a "benchmark in comics history." It was reprinted in Alter Ego magazine numbers 61 and 62.

His magazine work has been published in seven countries, and includes articles for Starlog, Jack & Jill and Star Trek, The Next Generation.

He briefly ghosted the internationally syndicated comic strip, Alley Oop, and created and wrote his own strip for five years called Holiday Out that was reprinted as a comic book. Vance also wrote comic book titles including *Straw Men, Angel of Death, The Adventures of Captain Nemo, Holiday Out* and *Bloodtide*. Artists with whom he has worked include, Wayne Truman, Richard "Grass" Green, and Dave (Alley Oop) Graue.

His work has appeared in several comic book anthologies, and he is listed in two reference works, the *Who's Who of American Comic Books* and *Comic Book Superstars*.

His thirty short stories about a fictional town called "Light's End" have been published in numerous magazines. They have also been recorded by legendary actor William (Murder She Wrote) Windom. One of these stories was nominated for the international 2004 SLF Fountain Award for Best Short Story.

These short stories were the foundation for a trilogy of novels published by Airship 27: *Weird Horror Tales, Weird Horror Tales: The Feasting*, and *Weird Horror Tales: Light's End*.

With novelists Mel Fox and R.A. Jones, he co-wrote *Global Star*, a tabloid in a world where werewolves and babies born with bowling balls in their stomachs are reality.

He co-wrote *The Equation*, a suspense-thriller about the impending financial collapse of America, with R. A. Jones.

Airship 27 also published Vance's novel, *Young Nemo and the Black Knights* about Jules Vern's Captain Nemo as a young man of eighteen years of age.

The Thief of Two Worlds is Vance's Middle Grade, Christian SF novel about a trip back into time to recover a 'jewel' of infinite value.

Vance's weekly comics review column, Suspended Animation, was continuously published for more than twenty years in fanzines, newspapers, and on over eighty websites. At its peak, it was read by approximately 4,000,000 readers a year. It was the longest, continuously published, comics review column in the world.

In his career, he worked in newspapers for twenty-two years as an editor, writer and advertising manager, creating three successful newspaper magazines. He also worked as an advertising copy writer, journalist, novelist, historian, graphic designer, in public relations, as a grant writer, cartoonist and columnist.

Vance also created the Oklahoma Cartoonists Collection housed in the Toy and Action Figure Museum in Pauls Valley, Oklahoma, and was a keynote speaker at the "Uncanny Adventures of Okie Cartoonists" exhibit at the Oklahoma Historical Museum in Oklahoma City He is a Christian.

INTERIOR ILLUSTRATOR

CHUCK BORDELL - was born a poor transistor farmer in the rust belt of western Pennsylvania. His childhood was filled with polluted rivers that he fell in love with anyway, the sound of railroad cars crashing together, and dreams of lusty women of dubious reputation. Eventually, he tired of all things iron and decided to trade rust for heavy metals, moving to Missoula, MT in 1987.

Despite a decided lack of tree cover (comparatively speaking) he found Missoula to his liking and, after earning a degree in Archaeology in 1991, decided to stay and continue his quest for the world record two-headed trout. In the meantime, he discovered that he had some skill in telling stories through sequential art and has since worked for numerous comic book publishers, including Malibu Comics, Caliber Comics, Alpha Productions and Silverline Comics. He has produced artwork for Steve Jackson Games and Dungeon Magazine, along with various illustrations for the Neverworld RPG and the Superdeck Superhero Card Game.

His most recent graphic novel is called Lunatic Fringe and recent gaming books include GURPS: Traveller and Earthdawn: Dragons. The Ministry of Wolves, a military fantasy, has just been published by SynergEbooks.

COVER ARTISTS –

COMPOSITON –

ROB DAVIS – Half of the partnership that is Airship 27 with Ron Fortier, Rob is the Art Director/Designer of Airship 27's books, and Pulp Factory Award-winning illustrator of same. Born and living in Missouri Rob has had a lifelong love of drawing and publishing, working in the Game and Comic Book worlds—working on books for Marvel, DC, Malibu, Innovation, Caliber and others from Merlin to Star Trek—before being happily coerced into book publishing by long-time friend and collaborator Ron Fortier. Look for Rob's illustrating stamp on interiors of the Robin Hood, Sherlock Holmes, Mystery Men (and Women), and Secret Agent "X" series, and others, at Airship 27 garnering Pulp Factory Award nominations for "best interior illustrations" nearly every year since their inception and winning in 2009. A simple gallery of Rob's work can be found at: robmdavis.com/gallery

COLORS –

SHANE EVANS – lives in small town Whangarei, New Zealand. He has one wife, two boys, two volkswagens and one insane dog.

He has been drawing, painting and creating since he can remember Inbetween the various illustration and airbrushing jobs, he has also been a graphic designer and signwriter. His style and tastes were greatly influenced by the steady diet of b-grade horror films, cult films and macho action movies. The comics that he grew up reading were 2000AD, The Savage Sword of Conan, Batman, Mad Magazine and others. Some of his favourite artists are Frank Frazetta, Simon Bisley, Dave McKean, John Buscemi and many many more.

You can look at his work online at: www.sevans.co.nz or on deviant art under the name SEVANS73.

And yes, he needs to post more work.

www.ingramcontent.com/pod-product-compliance
Lightning Source LLC
Chambersburg PA
CBHW071241250626
47163CB00001B/281